westermann

W0271184

CAMDEN ROAD

Workbook 6

Erarbeitet von:
Matthew Douglas (St. Catharines, ON, Canada)
Matthias Sitzmann (Schwandorf)

sowie Inga Birth (Köln) und Daniel Walker (Nidda)

Fachliche Beratung:
Andrea Lautenschlager (Passau)
Dr. Nina Leitz (Hof)
Sıtkı Özdemir (Fürth)
Sabine Pausch (Augsburg)
Dagmar Taylor (Edinburgh, Scotland)

Inhaltsverzeichnis

Auf den Seiten zu den einzelnen **Parts** findest du Aufgaben, die deine Englischfähigkeiten trainieren.

Auf den ***Challenge***-Seiten gibt es Aufgaben, die dich herausfordern können.

Mit den ***Check out***-Seiten kannst du weiter üben, wenn dir die *Check out*-Seiten im Textbook noch schwer gefallen sind oder, wenn du noch mehr trainieren möchtest. Im Anhang findest du die Lösungen zu diesen Aufgaben, damit du dich selbst überprüfen kannst.

Damit du die notwendige **Grammatik** immer schnell griffbereit hast, liegt diesem Workbook eine Übersicht (*Grammar in short*) bei, in der alle wichtigen Themen noch einmal kurz und knapp erklärt werden.

Es gibt zusätzlich ein eingelegtes Heftchen mit allen Lösungen.

Im Workbook findest du folgende Verweise:

1 grammar in short	Hier findest du Erklärungen und Beispiele im Grammatik-Einleger.

Dieses Symbol zeigt dir, dass es weiteres Material online gibt. Folgende Materialien sind verfügbar:

2 audio	Audiotrack zur Aufgabe
3 video	Video zur Aufgabe
DIGITAL+ portfolio	Portfolioseiten, auf denen du deine Fortschritte beim Englischlernen sehen kannst
DIGITAL+ wordbank	Vokabelaufgaben zu den Wordbanks im Textbook

Über diesen QR-Code gelangst du auf die Webseite
www.westermann.de/119007
Dort findest du alle Audiotracks und Zusatzmaterialien zum Workbook.

The first day after the holidays

1 skill: reading TB p. 164

Read the text on page 14 in your textbook again. Complete the sentences with information from the text.

0 Ben wants to talk about *what the class did in the summer holidays* .

1 In France, Ben ____________________ .

2 Emma spent her summer holiday ____________________ .

3 Emma has got photos of ____________________ .

4 Emma was sad because ____________________ .

5 Declan stayed at home and ____________________ .

6 Tia was late for school because ____________________ .

Declan's holidays

2 wordbank: holidays TB p. 177

Read what Declan says about his holidays. Fill in the right words.

My holidays were nice. I ____________________ *(↔* **go abroad***)* and spent a lot of time with my ____________________ *(ˈbrʌðə(r)z)*. On warm and ____________________ *(↔* **cloudy***)* days I met my friends in the park. We also went ____________________ () and we had lots of ____________________ *(ˌaɪs ˈkriːm)*. I played football with ____________________ () a few times as well. And we went to the ____________________ (). In the third week of the holidays, the weather in London was bad – really ____________________ *(↔* **warm***)* and ____________________ (). But it was OK – I had time to practise the ____________________ ().

Emma's photos

3a audio 1/4, skill: listening TB p. 163

Listen to Emma talking about her holiday photos. Put the photos in the right order (1–4).

3b

Choose one of the photos and describe it in complete sentences. Use the *present progressive* for all actions.

You can write:
In photo no. … I can see …
The people are …

Did they or didn't they?

4 grammar in short: 1 simple past

Write about what people did and didn't do in the holidays.

Emma

✗ stay in London
✓ visit Mount Snowdon
✗ take the train to the top

Declan

✗ go to France with Ben
✗ have bad weather
✓ meet Ben at the park

Tia and Jack

✓ go to Cyprus with their parents
✓ have a party on the beach
✗ have a picnic in the park

Emma didn't stay in London for the holidays. She visited …

Ben's survey

5 grammar in short: 2 simple past

Ben interviews Emma about her holidays. Read her answers and then write down Ben's questions.

Ben:

Emma: Yes, I did. I went to Wales.

Ben:

Emma: We went to Pembroke first and then to Snowdon National Park.

Ben: ______________________________

Emma: We visited a castle and the beach. And we ate lots of ice cream.

Ben: ______________________________

Emma: No, it wasn't. It was very rainy. But we had a bit of sun on some days.

Ben's results

6a

Look at Ben's class survey about the holidays. Are the statements right, wrong or not in the text? Tick (✓).

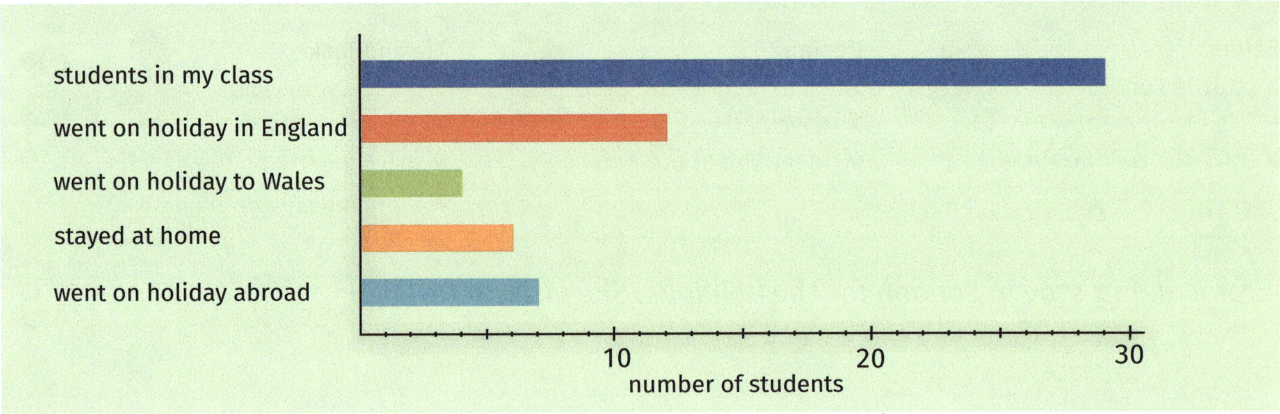

	right	wrong	not in the text
1 There are 27 students in Ben's class.	☐	☐	☐
2 Twelve students went on holiday in England.	☐	☐	☐
3 Only two students went on holiday to Wales.	☐	☐	☐
4 There are seven boys and 22 girls in Ben's class.	☐	☐	☐
5 Seven students went on holiday abroad.	☐	☐	☐
6 The bar chart shows that eight people stayed at home.	☐	☐	☐
7 Ben asked his classmates five questions.	☐	☐	☐
8 Eight students went on holiday to Scotland.	☐	☐	☐

6b

Correct the wrong statements.

____

____

____

____

This weekend

1 skill: reading TB p. 164

Read the text on page 18 in your textbook again. Tick (✓) the sentence which summarises the text best.

- ☐ Amy is planning her visit from Birmingham.
- ☐ Emma and her brother saw lots of London sights.
- ☐ Ben wants Emma to join him and Amy on a tour of the London sights.

Amy's trip to London

2a audio 1/6, skill: listening TB p. 163

Listen to Ben and Amy talking about Amy's trip to London. Are the statements right or wrong? Tick (✓).

	right	wrong
1 Amy is arriving by train from Birmingham on Thursday.	☐	☐
2 She likes the idea of a bus trip through London.	☐	☐
3 Amy wants to see Tower Bridge and the London Eye as well.	☐	☐
4 The bus tour starts at 10.30 a.m.	☐	☐
5 Ben is excited to go shopping at Covent Garden Market.	☐	☐
6 They want to take lots of photos at Madame Tussauds.	☐	☐
7 Amy is nervous about meeting Ben's friends.	☐	☐

2b

Amy found out about Tower Bridge and the London Eye. Read the information and answer the questions.

Tower Bridge, opened in 1894, is a bridge over the River Thames. You can watch it open when large ships need to pass through. You can visit all day, every day!

At 135 m high, the **London Eye** is the perfect place to get a great view of London! It opened in 2000 and you can visit every day from 11 a.m. to 6 p.m. It costs £30.50.

1 Where can you get a great view of the city? ____________
2 Which sight is the oldest? ____________
3 Which sight is open the longest? ____________
4 Which sight is best when you have no money? ____________

Sights and sounds

3 audio 1/8

What are these sights in London? Write them down. Then listen and check your answers.

1 Come to [ˌbɪg ˈben] with me. ____________
2 Let's relax in [ˌhaɪd ˈpɑːk]. ____________
3 We can go to [ˌkɒvənt ˈɡɑːdn]. ____________
4 I would enjoy a ride on the [ˌlʌndən‿ˈaɪ]. ____________
5 Let's have a look at beautiful [ˌbʌkɪŋəm ˈpæləs]. ____________
6 We could visit [ˌtaʊə ˈbrɪdʒ]. ____________
7 Why don't we go to the [ˌtaʊər‿əv ˈlʌndən] next? ____________

A London vlog

4a video 2, skill: understanding videos TB p. 169

Watch the vlog. While watching tick (✓) the right answer.
Jack and Emily are talking about ...

- [ ] ... the sights they want to visit in London.
- [ ] ... the sights they saw on their trip to London.

4b video 2

What do you remember? Circle the sights Jack and Emily went to.

Tower Bridge · Covent Garden · The Gherkin · Big Ben · the Tower of London · Hyde Park · the London Eye

4c video 2

Watch the vlog again and match the sentence parts. There is one more ending than you need.

1 Tower Bridge ☐
2 The Tower of London ☐
3 In the Jewel House at the Tower of London ☐
4 The Gherkin ☐
5 It has got 41 floors and ☐

A is London's most famous castle.
B is 180 metres tall.
C is 80 metres tall.
D opens up 1000 times every year.
E you can see the Crown Jewels.
F looks like an egg made of glass.

4d video 2

What are Emily's three favourite sights? Write them down.

1 ____________ 2 ____________ 3 ____________

Madame Tussauds

5 skill: mediation TB p. 166

Schaue dir die Webseite an und bearbeite die Aufgaben (1-4) stichpunktartig auf Deutsch. Ein Wort genügt nicht.

Madame Tussauds
Marylebone Road, London NW1 5LR

Visit this top tourist attraction with more than 250 lifelike wax figures, all designed with great detail. Meet the British Royal Family, say hello to sports legends and world leaders and come face to face with stars and superheroes. You are welcome to touch the figures and take photos with them. There is something new to discover every month.

Open daily from 10 a.m. – 4 p.m.
(The opening times can vary. Please check the Madame Tussauds official website for more information.)
Children under the age of 16 must be accompanied by a paying adult of 18+ years.

Buy tickets on our website by following this link: **TICKETS**

1 Was gibt es dort zu sehen? Nenne zwei Punkte.

____

2 Was kann man dort machen? Nenne zwei Punkte.

____

3 Was ist bei den Öffnungszeiten zu beachten?

____

4 Was wird über Kinder unter 16 Jahren gesagt?

____

At the weekend

6a grammar in short: 3+4 present progressive

Complete the email. Choose a verb from the box and put it in the *simple present* or *present progressive*.

stay · start · do · want · ~~write~~ · be · visit · have · go

New Message

To: camdenfriend@camdenroad.com

Subject: Hello from London :-)

Hi!
I _am writing_ you this email from our hotel in London! I _______ here with my mum. I usually _______ at home at the weekend, but this weekend we _______ the sights in London. Today we _______ to visit Buckingham Palace and go on a boat trip. Tomorrow evening we _______ to a show at the theatre. It _______ at 7.30 p.m. so we _______ an early dinner. What _______ you _______ this weekend?

Lots of love, Elliott xxx

6b

Answer Elliott's email. Write about your last visit to a city, say what you usually do and answer Elliott's question. Write about 50 words.

____

____

____

____

____

____

The way to London Zoo

1

skill: reading TB p. 164

Read the text on page 22 in your textbook again. Then tick (✓) the sentences right, wrong or not in the text.

	right	wrong	not in the text
1 Bill forgot to charge his phone last night.	☐	☐	☐
2 Ben knows how to get to London Zoo.	☐	☐	☐
3 London Zoo is on Prince Albert Road.	☐	☐	☐
4 Emma checks the way on her phone.	☐	☐	☐
5 London Zoo is close to Primrose Hill.	☐	☐	☐
6 To get to the zoo from Parkway, turn left into Prince Albert Road.	☐	☐	☐
7 The group is standing in Camden Market.	☐	☐	☐
8 Amy, Ben and Emma walked all the way to London Zoo.	☐	☐	☐

How do I get there?

2a

Read the three sets of directions. Start at Russell Square underground station and draw the routes on the map. Use three different colours.

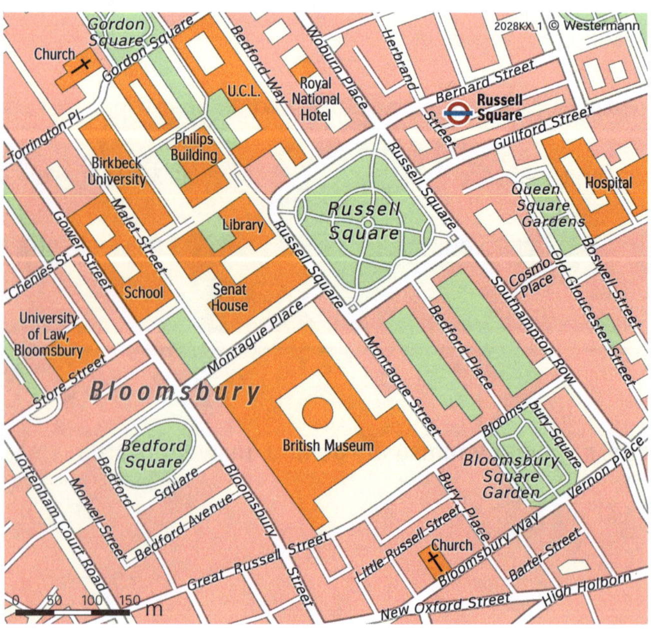

1 Start at Russell Square underground station. Turn left into Bernard Street. Walk straight on and then turn left into Russell Square. Go straight on to Southampton Row. Then turn left into Cosmo Place. Your destination is directly in front of you.

2 Start at Russell Square underground station. Turn left into Bernard Street. Walk straight on and then turn left into Russell Square. Go straight on to Southampton Row. Turn right into Great Russell Street. Walk straight on for a few minutes. Your destination is on your right.

3 Start at Russell Square underground station. Turn left into Bernard Street and go straight on. Then turn right into Woburn Place. Walk for a few minutes. Your destination is on your left.

2b

Match the directions from 2a and the destinations (A–D). There is one more destination than you need.

1 ________ 2 ________ 3 ________

A Royal National Hotel
B Queen Square Gardens
C Russell Square
D The British Museum

Sound check

3a audio 1/10

Listen to the sentences. Pay attention to the underlined letters. Then say them yourself.

1 Big Ben at the Palace of Westminster is world-famous.
2 Let's visit Covent Garden every day.
3 Walking through Hyde Park is very popular.
4 There are lots of bridges over the River Thames.
5 What can we watch today?
6 Every year there are millions of visitors to London.
7 When the weather is good, there are beautiful views from Primrose Hill.
8 You can visit the Crown Jewels in the Tower of London.

3b

Now sort the words from the box into the table.

world · every · Westminster · River · Covent · What · over · watch · we · visit

[/w/]	[/v/]

Which way?

4 audio 1/11, skill: listening TB p.163

Listen to the directions again. Match the people (1–3) and the things they say (A–F).

1 Speaker 1   2 Speaker 2   3 Speaker 3

A Turn left and walk down Station Lane. ☐
B Go straight on. The museum is on your right. ☐
C Go straight on down Park Avenue ... ☐
D Cross the road and walk along ... ☐
E Turn right into Wood Lane. ☐
F Walk past the café and turn left ... ☐

Lost in London

5 skill: mediation TB p.166

Du bist unterwegs in London. Eine deutsche Touristin hat sich verlaufen. Sie versteht den Londoner nicht, der versucht, ihr den Weg zu beschreiben. Erkläre der Touristin auf Deutsch, was der Londoner sagt.

1 **Londoner:** Walk straight on down the road. Then turn right into Nottingham Place.

1 **Du:**

2 **Londoner:** At the end of the street, turn left into Marylebone Road.
Madame Tussauds is across the road on your right.

2 **Du:**

Giving directions

6a video 3, skill: understanding videos TB p. 169

Watch the video and fill in the missing words.

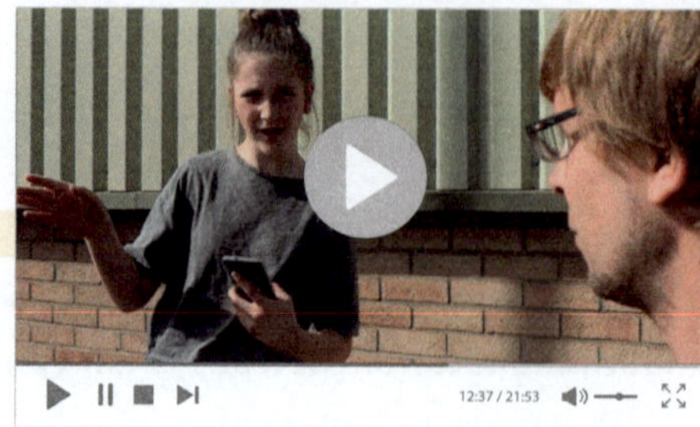

Thorsten: Hi, ______________ . Could you tell me how to get to ______________ , please?

Poppy: Yes. Take a ______________ down the Great North Road, then a ______________ down Almond Street. Walk for ______________ .

6b grammar in short: 5 imperative

Now look at these maps. Write directions for Max and Marlene. Use the words from the box.

go straight on · turn left · turn right · walk past ... · walk on until you get to ... · on your right · on your left · cross the street · ...

Excuse me, how do you get from Covent Garden Station to the London Transport Museum?

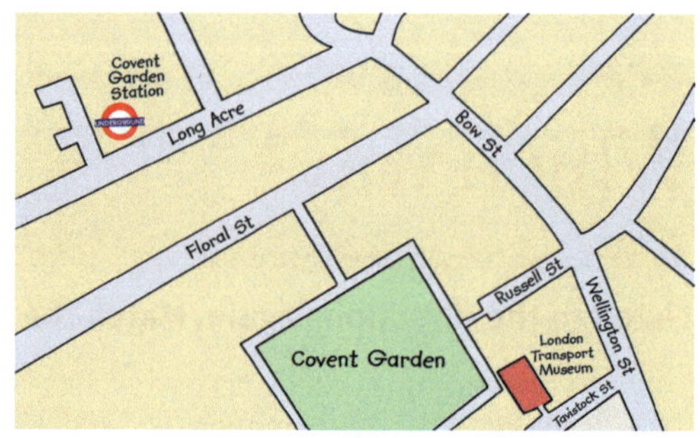

Turn left into ...

Can you help me, please? I'm at Baker Street Station and need to go to Weymouth Street.

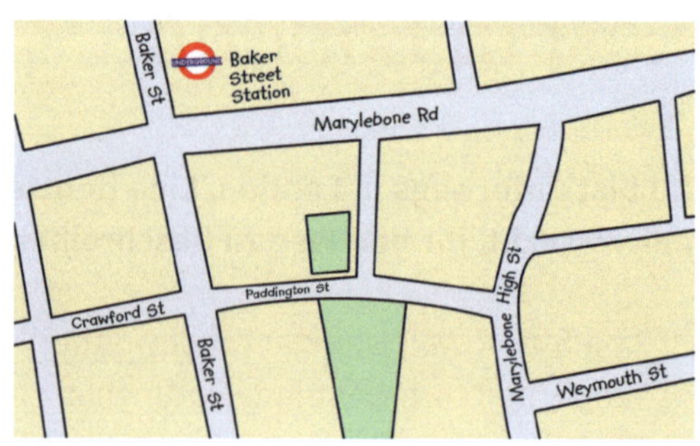

More about London sights

1a

Read the tips for sightseeing in London. Highlight adjectives and phrases in the texts that make a place sound interesting.

King's Cross Railway Station
Platform 9¾ at King 's Cross Railway Station is a "must-see" for all Harry Potter fans. That's where Harry caught the train to Hogwarts.

The Tower Bridge Glass Floor Walkway
Did you know that you can walk on a glass floor high up on Tower Bridge? Through the floor, you have a fantastic view of London below.

Covent Garden
Shops and stalls, acrobats and musicians – you can find them all at Covent Garden. Enjoy an exciting afternoon and watch, watch, watch!

Madame Tussauds
Experience one of London's best-loved attractions! Get up close and personal with your favourite stars and superheroes and take the selfie of a lifetime!

1b

Read the information about the sights. Match the information and the pictures.

Westminster Abbey
- large and famous church
- William and Kate got married here
- many kings and queens are buried here

☐

Harrods
- biggest department store in Europe
- sells everything, from golf clubs to yachts
- 35,000 visitors every day

☐

Arsenal museum
- in the stadium in North London
- see shirts, caps, medals from former players
- do a tour of the stadium

☐

1 

2 

3 

1c

Choose one of the sights from 1b. Use the information, the adjectives and the phrases from 1a to write a short text about it. Make it sound exciting.

Check out

Speaking solutions p.76

a) Work with a partner. Choose one of the pictures (1–9). Say what it means. Your partner points to the picture you described. Take turns.

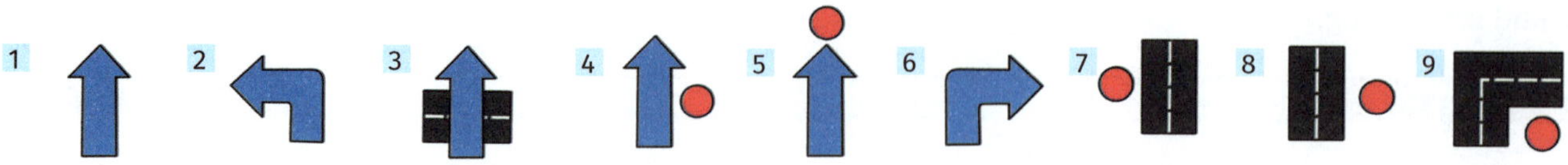

b) Look at the map. Give directions from St Marylebone Church to the Planetarium. Tell your partner. Use the phrases from a).

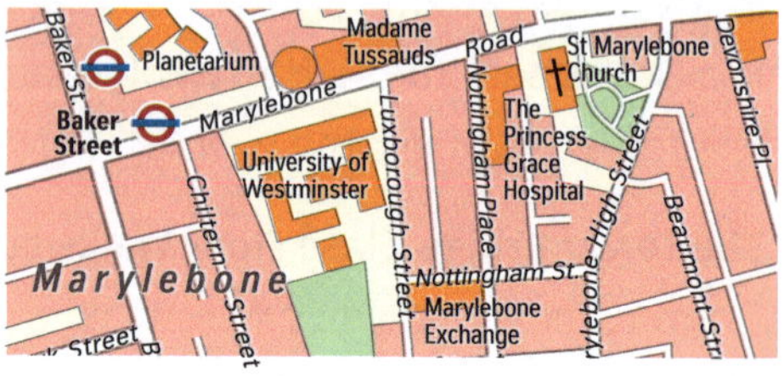

You can say:

Turn left …	*Go straight on …*
Turn right …	*…*

I can: give directions and use the imperative. ○

Writing solutions p.76

Write about five things you did in the last holidays.

In the holidays I ______________________

____

____

____

____

____

I can: write about holiday activities. ○

Listening audio 1/15, solutions p.76

Listen to Tim. Tick (✓) all the things he did in the holidays.

- ☐ spend a lot of time at home
- ☐ go to London Zoo
- ☐ watch a film at the cinema
- ☐ play volleyball at Hyde Park
- ☐ eat vanilla ice cream

I can: understand somebody talking about holidays. ○

Mediation solutions p.76

Lies dir das Schild durch. Ergänze die fehlenden Informationen im deutschen Infotext.

Facts about Buckingham Palace
- The palace has got 775 rooms, including 78 bathrooms.
- Some of the rooms are open to visitors in summer.
- At Buckingham Palace there are royal parties.
- Lots of royal children were born at the palace.

Der Buckingham Palast hat ______________ Räume. Im ______________ können Besucher den Palast besichtigen. Im Palast werden ______________ veranstaltet. Viele königliche ______________ wurden im Palast geboren.

I can: summarise important information on a sign in German. ○

Reading solutions p. 76

Read Boris' postcard. Answer the questions about it. Take notes.

Hello from sunny London!
I am having a great time here. London is such a cool city. We did a bus tour yesterday. We saw all the famous sights - Buckingham Palace, the London Eye, Hyde Park and more. Today we are going shopping. I want to buy some souvenirs at Camden Market. Tomorrow we want to go to the British Museum to learn about history. It's one of the free museums.
Best wishes, Boris

1 Where is Boris? ______
2 What is the weather like? ______
3 What does he think of London? ______
4 What did he see yesterday? ______
5 Where is he going today? ______
6 Why are they going to the museum? ______

I can: understand what somebody says about their holidays. ◯

USE OF ENGLISH

Grammar solutions p. 76

What did Melody do in the holidays? What didn't she do? Write sentences. Use the *simple past*.

0  ✓
1  ✓
2  ✗
3  ✗

0 *She went swimming with her friends.*
1 ______
2 ______
3 ______

Vocabulary solutions p. 76

Sort the words and phrases from the box into the table.

visit family · Hyde Park · turn right · cold · meet friends · Covent Garden · cross the street · go to the park · rainy · the Tower of London · warm · on the left

holiday activities	weather words	directions	places in London

I can: talk about things in the past. ◯ use words from the word field "holidays". ◯

The Big Issue

1 skill: reading TB p.164

Read the text on page 34 in your textbook again. Tick (✓) the sentences right, wrong or not in the text.

	right	wrong	not in the text
1 Bianca grew up in London.	☐	☐	☐
2 Before she lost her job, Bianca lived in a big flat.	☐	☐	☐
3 "The Big Issue" is a free magazine.	☐	☐	☐
4 The people at the homeless shelter were good for Bianca.	☐	☐	☐
5 All homeless people sleep in underground stations.	☐	☐	☐
6 Spending time with Bailey is the best thing about Bianca's job.	☐	☐	☐

The London Tube

2a skill: mediation TB p.166

Lies den Artikel über die *London Tube*, den du in der Zeitschrift "The Big Issue" gefunden hast. Bearbeite die Aufgaben stichpunktartig auf Deutsch. Ein Wort genügt nicht.

Dusty explains

1 million = 1 Million
1 billion = 1 Milliarde

The London Tube

The London Tube opened in 1863. It's the oldest underground railway system in the world and the very first that was electrified. It's called "the underground", but half of the Tube runs above the ground. Many years ago, smoking was allowed in the stations and trains, but that changed in 1987 when smoking was banned because of a fire. Today the Tube has more than 4100 trains and around 270 stations. 1.35 billion people use it every year, about two to three million every day, sometimes many more. The busiest station is Waterloo with about a hundred million passengers every year. 23 escalators bring passengers down to the trains and up to the streets.
As London's roads are full of taxis, buses and cars, the Tube is the fastest way to travel around London. Trains can travel at up to 62 miles per hour – that's 100 kilometres an hour.

1 Was war an der U-Bahn so besonders zu der Zeit, als sie eröffnet wurde?

2 Was änderte sich 1987 und warum?

3 Wieviele Passagiere nutzen heutzutage die U-Bahn pro Jahr?

4 Was erfährt man über die Waterloo Station? (Nenne drei Aspekte.)

5 Warum ist die Tube das schnellste Verkehrsmittel in London? (Nenne zwei Gründe.)

2b

What is the most interesting fact about the London Tube? Explain your answer. If there is none, say why.

You can write:
I find it interesting that … because it's so old / so many people use it / …

How to use an Oyster Card

3 audio 1/20, skill: listening TB p. 163

Listen to the tourist and answer the questions. You do not have to write complete sentences, but one word is not enough.

1 What is an Oyster Card for?

2 Where can you use it? Name three means of transport.

3 What do you do with the card at the start of your journey?

4 Why should you use the Oyster Card?

5 How do you put money on an Oyster Card?

6 Where can you get an Oyster Card?

Was or were?

4 grammar in short: 1 simple past

Do you remember the *simple past* forms of *to be*? Complete the sentences with the correct forms.

0 Last week, we *were* (✓) in London.

1 ______ (✓) you on a school trip?

2 My friend was sick on the way to London. The teachers ______ (✗) very happy.

3 I didn't see you on the bus. You ______ (✗) there.

4 ______ (✓) you on the trip to the zoo last month? I ______ (✗) because I ______ (✓) ill that day.

5 Me and my friend ______ (✗) on the trip either.

On the way to Big Ben

5 grammar in short: 6+7 past progressive, wordbank: London TB p. 178

Yesterday you were on the way to Big Ben. Play the game with a partner and tell them about your trip.

You need: a dice *(Würfel)* and a playing piece (a coin, rubber, small figure, ...)
How to play the game:

- Start in Camden. Roll the dice. Move your playing piece forward the right number of spaces.
- Read the text on the space where you land. Form a statement (✓), a negative statement (✗) or a question (?), e.g. "I was going into the station". If you ask a question, your partner must give an answer. Use the *past progressive*. If you land on a picture, describe what you can see.
- Then it is your partner's turn. The first player to reach Big Ben is the winner.

	go into the station ✓		look for my Oyster Card ✓	talk to people ?
eat a sandwich ?	play on my smartphone ✗	watch other people ✓	open the window ?	listen to music ✗
read a magazine ✓	meet friends ?	get off the train ✓		wait for a bus ?
use a map on my phone ✗		look for a taxi ✗	talk loudly ?	walk over the bridge ✗
walk along the river ✓	sit in the park ✓	feed the ducks ✗	go to the London Eye ✗	
	feel excited ?	take photos ✓		wait for a boat trip ?

The Brixton Food Festival

1a skill: reading TB p. 164

Read the text on page 38 in your textbook again. Match the sentence halves.

1 At the festival there is food from ...
2 On Saturday afternoon you can ...
3 On the festival's website you can find ...
4 You can get to the food festival ...
5 Visitors can bring their dogs ...
6 If you have questions, you can ...

☐ learn how to cook dishes without meat.
☐ if they keep them on a lead.
☐ more information about the events and the festival area.
☐ all corners of the world.
☐ call or email the people who are organising the festival.
☐ by bus, train or Tube.

1b

Some tourists want to visit the festival. Answer their questions with information from the text on page 38 in your textbook. You do not have to write complete sentences, but one word is not enough.

1 Sam: I don't eat meat and I don't like fish. What can I eat there?
2 Lucy: I have to work until 6 p.m. Can I still listen to the live music? Why?
3 Luke: I want to bring my children, but Tilly is still a baby. Where can I find changing facilities?
4 Brad: I can only come on Friday. What programme highlights are there for me?

1 ______________________
2 ______________________
3 ______________________
4 ______________________

When / while I was at the festival

2 grammar in short: 6+7 past progressive

Read the sentences and circle the right form of the verb.

1 My grandma **was calling / called** me when I **was walking / walked** to the festival.
2 I **was talking / talked** to my friend when I **was seeing / saw** my English teacher at the festival.
3 My friends **were listening / listened** to the band while I **was standing / stood** in the queue for the burgers.
4 When my mum **was looking for / looked for** me, I **was buying / bought** a burger.
5 While we **were finishing / finished** our curry, the organisers **were cleaning / cleaned** up.

A pizza recipe

3a

Look at the recipe for margherita pizza. Underline the ingredients in blue and the tools you need in yellow.

Dusty explains

In recipes you often find short forms: tsp = teaspoon(s), tbsp = tablespoon(s) and mins = minutes.

MARGHERITA PIZZA

★★★★★ 58 ratings | 30 minutes | easy | 2–4 | £ cheap

INGREDIENTS

Dough
500g flour
1 tsp yeast
1 tsp sugar
1 tsp salt
1 ½ tsp olive oil

Tomato sauce
500 ml passata
1 tsp fresh basil
½ tsp dried oregano
1 garlic clove

Topping
2 tomatoes (thinly sliced)
200 g mozzarella cheese
fresh basil leaves
chilli oil

STEPS

1. Put the flour, yeast and sugar in a large bowl. Add 300 ml of lukewarm water and mix together. Add the oil and salt. Stir well until it forms a soft and sticky dough. If it's too dry, add a little bit of cold water.
2. Put some flour on the work surface and knead the dough for 10 mins. Put it back in the bowl, cover it with a tea towel and leave it to rise for 1 hour.
3. Heat the oven to 220°C and place a baking tray in the oven to heat up.
4. Knead the dough again and then leave it while you make the sauce.
5. To make the sauce, put all of the ingredients into a bowl. Add some salt, pepper and a pinch of sugar. Then mix well.
6. Now take the dough and divide it into 2 or 4 pieces (for 2 big pizzas or 4 small ones). Shape the pieces into balls and then flatten them to make thin circles.
7. Put some flour on the hot baking tray and then the dough circles. Spread 4–5 tbsp of sauce on each circle. Then add the tomato slices, the cheese and some olive oil. Bake the pizzas in the oven for 10–12 mins or until the cheese melts and is golden brown.
8. Decorate the pizzas with the fresh basil leaves. Add some chilli oil if you like your pizza spicy. Serve and enjoy!

3b

Lies dir das Rezept noch einmal durch. Bringe die Schritte in die richtige Reihenfolge.

☐ Knete den Teig 10 Minuten lang.

☐ Mische die Zutaten für die Sauce zusammen.

☐ Verstreiche die Sauce auf dem Teig (4–5 EL pro Pizza), verteile dann die Tomatenscheiben und den Käse.

☐ Gib das Mehl, die Hefe und den Zucker in eine Schüssel. Füge Wasser, Öl und Salz hinzu.

☐ Lass den Teig ca. 1 Stunde gehen.

☐ Knete den Teig noch einmal.

☐ Teile den Teig in 2–4 Stücke und rolle ihn zu dünnen Kreisen aus.

☐ Backe die Pizzas bis der Käse schmilzt. Streue die Basilikum-Blätter darauf. Guten Appetit!

3c

What are these German words in English? Find them in the recipe and write them down.

1 Teig ______
4 backen ______
7 servieren ______
2 kneten ______
5 Zutaten ______
8 Backblech ______
3 Schüssel ______
6 hinzufügen ______
9 rühren ______

2b skill: writing TB p. 165

Imagine you are Holly. Write her answer to Matilda. You should write about 50 words.

You should:
- thank Matilda for her email.
- say something to make her feel better.
- write what you think about her problem.
- say what you think she should do.

Include:
- Salutation: "Dear ...,"
- Introduction: What is the topic of the email?
- Body: Main points in a logical order
- Closing sentence
- Signing off: "Best wishes, ..." or "From ..."

New Message

To: matilda@brighton.com

Subject: RE: Problems with my sister!

Zara's challenge

3a video 7, skill: understanding videos TB p. 169

Watch the video. What is Zara's challenge?

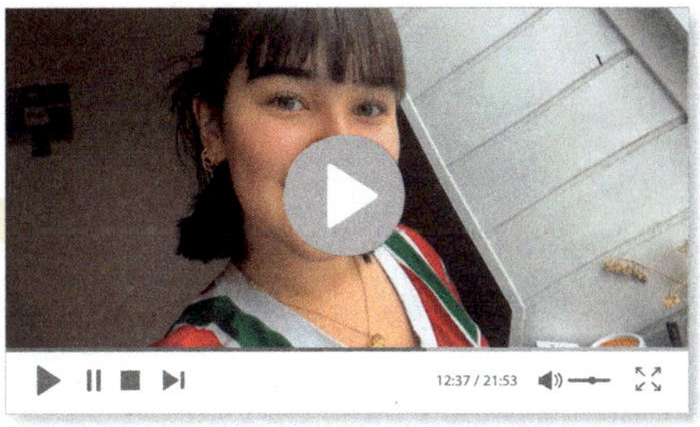

3b video 7, skill: understanding videos TB p. 169

Watch the video again. Write down four difficult situations that Zara faces. How does she solve her problems?

Difficult situations:		Solutions:
1	→	1
2	→	2
3	→	3
4	→	4

3c

Look at the questions. Think about your answers and then talk to a partner. You can make notes in your exercise book.

1 Do you think it would be a good idea to write down your friends' telephone numbers? Explain your answer.
2 What would you do if wanted to go somewhere but didn't know how to get there without a phone?
3 Is it important to know how to use a library? Explain your answer.
4 Is it important to have handwriting *(Handschrift)* that others can read? What could it be important for?
5 Could you imagine doing a challenge like Zara? Explain your answer.

Which word?

4 grammar in short: 8 quantifiers

Complete the sentences with *much*, *many*, *a lot of* or *lots of*. There is more than one possible answer.

1 My friend has ______________ followers.
2 I don't spend ______________ time on social media. Maybe that is the problem!
3 I don't want to share ______________ information about my life online.
4 My privacy is more important to me than getting ______________ likes.

Much and many, some and any

5a grammar in short: 8 quantifiers

Read the article and circle the right word.

Less screen time, more real time

How **many / a lot of** hours do you spend online every day? **Any / Some** people spend **many / a lot of** time on the internet. They like to share **many / much** things about their lives with their friends online. But people sometimes don't realise how **much / many** personal information they are sharing when they do this. **Lots of / Many** what people post is visible to everyone on the internet. That is why there are often **much / many** comments from people they don't know, and **any / some** people don't write nice things. The internet is very useful for **much / a lot of** things, but it is not always good for us. Internet users should make sure that they don't share **some / any** personal information online. If there is a problem, there are **much / lots of** experts who can give people **many / lots of** advice. And, of course, it is a great idea to take **many/ much** breaks from being online. Have a think: can you make **much / any** changes to how you use the internet?

5b

Complete the sentences. Choose the correct words from exercise 6b on page 45 in your textbook.

1 I don't have ______________ ideas for my post. Can ______________ help me?
2 I thought there was a fly in my photo, but there's just ______________ on my screen.
3 I need a place for a selfie but can't find ______________ . I can look for ______________ later.

A very short history of communication

1a

Look at the pictures (1–7). Then match them and the texts about the history of communication.

1

2

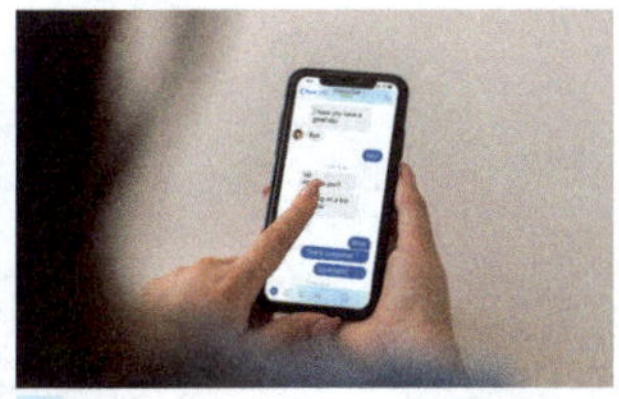

3

4

5

6

7

In 1876 Alexander Graham Bell invented the telephone. Now people could talk to each other – even in different countries. ☐

Now computers are everywhere. We use the internet to get information from all over the world and send emails in seconds. ☐

People could buy the first smartphones in 2007. These small computers changed the way we communicate. ☐

In the Stone Age large groups of people lived together in caves. They made sounds and signs with their hands. The sounds became words. In different parts of the world people made different sounds. That's why we have different languages. ☐

About 5,000 years ago, the Egyptians invented papyrus – the first kind of paper. They also invented hieroglyphics – special symbols which were the first letters. ☐

600 years ago, people in Europe started to write letters which messengers brought to the right address. This early kind of post was good, but not very fast. It took two weeks for a letter to get from England to Italy. ☐

In the 20th century there were thousands of new inventions, including the computer. The first computer was as big as a room. ☐

1b

Go online and find out three more facts about the first telephone, computer and smartphone. Make notes.

The first telephone	*The first computer*	*The first smartphone*
1.	1.	1.
2.	2.	2.
3.	3.	3.

invented = *erfand*; Stone Age = *Steinzeit*; cave = *Höhle*; Egyptians = *Ägypter*; hieroglyphics = *Hieroglyphen*; messengers = *Boten*; inventions = *Erfindungen*

Check out

Speaking solutions p. 77

Talk to a partner. What were the people doing at the Tube station yesterday at 4 p.m.? Take turns.

You can say:

P1: The woman with the red hair was thinking about …
P2: Bianca was selling the "Big Issue".
P1: The boys were talking about …
P1: …

I can: talk about people at a Tube station. ◯

Listening audio 1/26, solutions p. 77

Listen to Terry. Find and correct the mistakes.

0 Terry went to the food festival ~~last week~~. *yesterday*

1 Terry and Louis had food from at least 10 different countries.

2 The cake was made with chocolate and cheese.

3 It was interesting to learn about Italian cooking.

4 Louis liked the insects best.

5 Terry and Louis are not coming back next year.

I can: understand a report. ◯

Reading solutions p. 77

Complete the text with the sentences (A–E). There are more letters than you need.

The most important rule is: never share personal information online. You should also be careful when posting photos. ☐ Always think before you post. Don't post a picture of someone else without asking them. ☐ Imagine how you would feel! Always remember: ☐ So when you comment on something be polite. ☐ You can use emojis to help other people understand what you mean.

A They might not want to have the photo online.
B Make sure you post every day.
C It can be difficult to know how you mean things.
D Words can be very rude and hurtful.
E Maybe the photos show your house or street?

I can: understand a text about social media. ◯

Writing solutions p. 77

Yesterday you went to a food festival. Write a short email to a friend and tell them about it. Write about 50 words and tell your friend:

- where the festival was.
- how you got there and who you went with.
- what food you ate / liked / didn't like.

Use your exercise book.

I can: write about a food festival. ◯

Mediation
solutions p. 77

Lies den Infotext über die *Big Issue*. Korrigiere die Fehler in den deutschen Sätzen.

> **The "Big Issue"**
> Interested in selling The "Big Issue"? Here's how to start:
> 1. Always make an appointment at one of our offices.
> 2. Tell us about yourself and we'll explain the next steps.
> 3. If selling The "Big Issue" is the right thing for you, you'll get a "Big Issue" outfit (so that people know you're an official vendor) and 10 free magazines.
>
> *How does it work again?* After your 10 free magazines, you buy magazines from us for £2 each and sell them on for £4, keeping the profit for yourself.
> Sound good? Get in touch!

1 Man braucht keinen Termin, um anzufangen.

____

2 Verkäufer sollen ihre eigene Kleidung tragen.

____

3 Verkäufer kaufen die ersten 10 Zeitschriften zum halben Preis.

____

4 Die Verkäufer verdienen £4 pro Zeitschrift.

____

I can: understand important information in an English text. ◯

USE OF ENGLISH

Grammar
solutions p. 77

What were the people doing last Monday at 4 p.m.? Fill in the verbs in the *past progressive*.

0 Terry ___was listening to___ (listen to) the famous chef's talk.

1 The chef ______________ (explain) how to make scrambled eggs from tofu.

2 Louis ______________ (not eat) spicy insects.

3 We ______________ (talk) about the "Big Issue".

4 My parents ______________ (ask) about the school trip.

Vocabulary
solutions p. 77

Underline the wrong word and think of a suitable word for each line.

0 Keiko's mum, Ella, works in a restaurant. She prepares meals for guests. She is a doctor. ___cook___

1 At the restaurant you can eat many vegan dishes. They are without meat but often have cheese and eggs in them. ______________

2 Bianca and Bailey don't have their own place to live. They are jobless. ______________

3 Mike doesn't have a job, but he is hopeless he can soon find work again. ______________

4 When you eat a picture of someone on social media, you should ask him or her if it's OK. ______________

I can: write about things happening in the past. ◯ use important words. ◯

Class trip reports

1a skill: reading TB p. 164

Read text A on page 54 in your textbook again. Tick (✓) the sentences right, wrong or not in the text.

	right	wrong	not in the text
1 Heathrow is the biggest airport in Northern Ireland.	☐	☐	☐
2 The bus to Belfast is less expensive than the plane.	☐	☐	☐
3 Belfast is the capital of Northern Ireland.	☐	☐	☐
4 The Giant's Causeway is 55 miles away from Belfast.	☐	☐	☐
5 The Coleraine Walks is a historical walking path.	☐	☐	☐
6 The Edge Watersports Park is expensive.	☐	☐	☐
7 The weather was sunny the whole trip.	☐	☐	☐

1b

Read text B on page 54 in your textbook again and complete the sentences with information from the text.

1 Class 8CK went on a trip to ______________________ .

2 They went there by ______________________ .

3 The journey there took ______________________ .

4 It was not easy for the students ______________________ .

5 The guide spoke ______________________ .

6 Ben Nevis is ______________________ .

7 Some of the students tasted ______________________ .

1c

Read text C on page 55 in your textbook again and tick (✓) the correct boxes .

1 Where did the class travel to?	St Michael's Mount	☐	St Austell	☐	Falmouth	☐
2 Where did they stay?	hotel	☐	hostel	☐	with families	☐
3 When did they go?	first half of year	☐	in the summer	☐	second half of year	☐
4 What was their favourite town?	Falmouth	☐	Truro	☐	Mevagissey	☐
5 What was their favourite sight?	Eden Project	☐	King Arthur	☐	Truro	☐

My day in the UK

2 skill: writing TB p. 165

Read the texts on pages 54 / 55 in your textbook again. Imagine you visited one of the places in the texts. Write a diary entry about it. You can do some research first. Write about 60 words. You can write about:

1 where you went
2 what you did
3 how you liked it
4 a funny moment

A museum in Northern Ireland

3 skill: mediation TB p. 166

Du bist in einem Museum in Nordirland. Im deutschen Museumsführer gibt es ein Rätsel. Um es lösen zu können, musst du den Text auf der Infotafel lesen. Verbinde dann die Satzteile und finde das Lösungswort.

The Titanic Museum in Belfast

The Titanic Museum Belfast opened in 2012, almost exactly one hundred years after the RMS Titanic sank. The ship hit an iceberg on its first journey to New York City in 1912. The building is close to the shipyard on Queen's Island where the Titanic was built. Its form reflects the shape of the ship itself as well as the iceberg. Belfast locals sometimes even call it "The Iceberg".
There are several galleries within the museum. Inside, you can go on a carriage that takes you on a ride through scenes of the ship's construction between 1909 and 1911. You can also listen to audios of survivors and even watch videos of what the Titanic looks like today, which lies almost 3800 metres deep in the North Atlantic.

1 Die Eröffnung des Museums
2 Auf seiner ersten Fahrt
3 Das Museum
4 Viele Belfaster
5 Im Museum
6 In Audioaufnahmen
7 Das Wrack der Titanic

R nennen das Gebäude „Eisberg".
E erzählen Überlebende ihre Geschichten.
O hat das Schiff einen Eisberg gerammt.
N kann man auf einer Fahrt über den Bau des Schiffes lernen.
J war fast genau 100 Jahre nach dem Sinken des Schiffes.
Y liegt fast 3.800 Meter tief im Meer.
U befindet sich in der Nähe der Werft, wo die Titanic gebaut wurde.

1	
2	
3	
4	
5	
6	
7	

Comparing places

4a grammar in short: 9 comparison of adjectives

Look at the pictures and find adjectives in the box that describe them. You can also think of other adjectives. Then compare the things in the pictures.

United Kingdom	Germany	Bavaria

delicious · beautiful · nice · big · interesting · cute · old · healthy · ...

0 *Fish and chips is as delicious as "Weißwurst".*

1 ____________________.

2 ____________________.

3 ____________________.

4 ____________________.

5 ____________________.

4b grammar in short: 9 comparison of adjectives

Fill in the right forms of the adjectives.

0 Berlin is far away, but London is *further* away and Belfast is *furthest* away.

1 In Germany the weather is bad today, in England it is ____________ but in Scotland it is the ____________.

2 There is little traffic in Cardiff and in York there is even ____________, but the ____________ traffic is on the island Herm.

3 Many people live in Ireland, but ____________ people live in England and the ____________ people live in Germany.

Unit 1

Part A: After the holidays

Back to school (Seite 4)
1: 1 camped, hiked and swam with his family. **2** in Wales on a hiking holiday. **3** the beach. **4** her brother went back to Germany **5** helped look after his brothers **6** she didn't hear her alarm

Declan's holidays (Seite 4)
2: 1 stayed at home **2** brothers **3** sunny **4** swimming **5** ice cream **6** Ben **7** cinema **8** cold **9** rainy **10** drums

Emma's photos (Seite 4-5)
3a: 4, 2, 1, 3
3b: Individuelle Lösung

Did they or didn't they (Seite 5)
4: *Emma didn't stay in London for the holidays. She visited* Mount Snowdon. Emma didn't take the train to the top. Tia and Jack went to Cyprus with their parents. They had a party on the beach. They didn't have a picnic at the park. Declan didn't go to France with Ben. He didn't have bad weather. Declan met Ben at the park.

Ben's survey (Seite 5-6)
5: 1 Did you go somewhere on holiday? **2** Where did you go in Wales? **3** What did you do? **4** Was the weather nice?

Ben's results (Seite 6)
6a: 1 wrong **2** right **3** wrong **4** not in the text **5** right **6** wrong **7** wrong **8** not in the text
6b: 1 There are twenty-nine students **3** Four students went on holiday to Wales **6** Six people stayed at home **7** Ben asked four questions

Part B: London sights

This weekend (Seite 7)
1: Ben wants Emma to join him and Amy on a tour of the London sights

Amy's trip to London (Seite 7)
2a: 1 right **2** right **3** wrong **4** wrong **5** wrong **6** right **7** right
2b: 1 The London Eye **2** Tower Bridge **3** Tower Bridge **4** Tower Bridge

Sights and sounds (Seite 12)
3: 1 Big Ben **2** Hyde Park **3** Covent Garden **4** London Eye **5** Buckingham Palace **6** Tower Bridge **7** Tower of London

A London vlog (Seite 8)
4a: the sights they saw on their trip to London
4b: Tower Bridge, The Gherkin, the Tower of London, Hyde Park
4c: 1 D **2** A **3** E **4** B **5** F
4d: the Tower of London, Hyde Park, The Gherkin

Madame Tussauds (Seite 8-9)
5: 1 Man kann Wachsfiguren von Sportlern und Superhelden sehen **2** Man kann die Figuren anfassen und Fotos machen **3** Sie können variieren **4** Sie müssen von einem Erwachsenen begleitet werden

At the weekend (Seite 9)
6a: Hi! I am writing you this email from our hotel room in London! I *am* here with my mum. I usually *stay* at home at the weekend, but this weekend we *are visiting* the sights in London. Today we *want* to visit Buckingham Palace and go on a boat trip. Tomorrow evening we *are going* to a show at the theatre. It *starts* at 7.30 p.m. so we *are having* an early dinner. What *are* you *doing* this weekend?
6b: Individuelle Lösung

Part C: Giving directions
The way to London Zoo (Seite 10)
1: **1** wrong. **2** right **3** right **4** right **5** right **6** wrong **7** wrong **8** not in the text

How do I get there? (Seite 10)
2a: Individuelle Lösung
2b: 1 B **2** D **3** A

Sound check (Seite 11)
3a: Individuelle Lösung
3b: w - world, Westminster, what, watch, we
v - every, River, Covent, over, visit

Which way? (Seite 11)
4: A 1 **B** 3 **C** 2 **D** 3 **E** 1 **F** 2

Lost in London (Seite 11)
5: 1 Gehen Sie geradeaus die Straße hinunter. Biegen Sie dann rechts in den Nottingham Place ein. **2** Am Ende der Straße biegen Sie links in die Marylebone Road ein. Madame Tussauds liegt auf der anderen Straßenseite auf der rechten Seite.

Giving directions (Seite 12)
6a: excuse me, the library, left, right, five minutes
6b: 1 Turn left into Long Acre. Then turn right into Bow Street and go straight on. Turn right into Tavistock Street. The London Transport Museum is on your right.
2 Turn left into Baker Street and then right into Marylebone Road. Go straight on and then cross the street at Marylebone High Street. Turn right into Marylebone High Street. Walk straight on until you get to Weymouth Street. It is on your left.

Challenge (Seite 13)
More about London sights
1a: Individuelle Lösung
1b: 1 Harrods **2** Arsenal museum **3** Westminster Abbey
1c: Beispiel: Harrods is a "must-see" for anyone who likes shopping. It is the biggest department store in Europe! You can buy your favourite thing here as they sell everything. It is a best-loved place, with 35,000 visitors every day!

Checkout (Seite 14–15)
Speaking: Individuelle Lösung
Writing: Individuelle Lösung
Listening: spend a lot of time at home, go to London Zoo, play volleyball at Hyde Park
Mediation: 1 775 **2** Sommer **3** Feiern **4** Kinder
Reading: 1 in London **2** It is sunny. **3** He thinks it's cool. **4** Buckingham Palace, London Eye, Hyde Park / lots of famous sights **5** shopping at Camden Market **6** to learn about history
Grammar: 1 She baked a cake. / She ate cake. **2** She didn't paint. **3** She didn't go to a museum / an art gallery.
Vocabulary: holiday activities visit family, meet friends, go to the park **weather words** cold, rainy, warm **directions** turn right, cross the street, on the left **places in London** Hyde Park, Covent Garden, the Tower of London

Unit 2

Part A: The streets of London
The Big Issue (Seite 16)
1: 1 right **2** not in the text **3** wrong
4 not in the text **5** wrong **6** right

The London Tube (Seite 16-17)
2a: 1 Es war das erste unterirdische Eisenbahnsystem, das elektrisch betrieben wurde **2** Das Rauchen war nicht mehr erlaubt wegen eines Feuers **3** 1,35 Milliarden Leute **4** Station mit dem meisten Verkehr, 100 Millionen Passagiere jedes Jahr, 23 Rolltreppen **5** überirdisch sind die Straßen voll, die Tube fährt 100km/h
2b: Individuelle Lösung

How to use an Oyster Card (Seite 17)
3: 1 for travelling in London **2** bus, Tube, tram, boat and train **3** tap it on the card reader **4** It saves you money. **5** at special machines in the stations **6** online or at a ticket shop

Was or were? (Seite 17)
4: 1 were **2** weren't **3** weren't **4** were, wasn't, was **5** weren't

On the way to Big Ben (Seite 18)
5: Individuelle Lösung

Part B: Colourful London
The Brixton Food Festival (Seite 19)
1a: 1 all corners of the world **2** learn how to cook dishes without meat **3** more information about the events and the festival area **4** by bus, train or Tube **5** if they keep them on a lead **6** call or email the people who are organising the festival.
1b: 1 curry, vegetables, tofu **2** yes, the music goes on til 10pm **3** next to the main stage **4** live music

When/while I was at the festival (Seite 19)
2: 1 called, was walking **2** was talking, saw **3** were listening, was standing **4** was looking, was buying **5** were finishing, were cleaning

A pizza recipe (Seite 20)
3a: Ingredients: flour, yeast, sugar, lukewarm water, oil, salt, cold water, pepper, tomato slices, cheese, olive oil, basil leaves, chilli oil
Tools: large bowl, tea towel, oven, baking tray
3b: 2, 7, 3, 6, 5, 1, 4, 8
3c: 1 dough **2** to knead **3** bowl **4** to bake **5** ingredients **6** to add **7** to serve **8** baking tray **9** to stir

Restaurant reviews (Seite 21)
4a: Individuelle Lösung
4b: Individuelle Lösung

Crossword puzzle (Seite 21)
5a: 1 delicious **2** recipe **3** flavour **4** restaurant **5** Borough **6** spicy **7** while **8** vegetarian **9** curry
solution word: diversity
5b: Having a range of different things

Part C: Media
A funny photo? (Seite 22)
1a: Declan gets help with his problem
1b: 1 shared them online **2** he had an allergic reaction **3** lots of people could see **4** some privacy **5** she's good at sorting out problems **6** ask to take down the photo

Matilda's email (Seite 22-23)
2a: 1 older-younger **2** do anything to help-listen **3** asks-doesn't ask **4** Matilda's-Zoe's
2b: Individuelle Lösung

Zara's challenge (Seite 23-24)
3a: 1 Low-tech challenge (for one week)
3b: Difficult situations: **1** can't chat with her friend about a birthday present

2 can't look up directions **3** can't use the internet for homework **4** has bad handwriting / can't use laptop for book report
Solutions: **1** think of a present herself **2** look at signs / ask people **3** go to the library **4** use her granddad's typewriter
3c: Individuelle Lösung

Which word? (Seite 24)
4: 1 a lot of / lots of / many **2** much / a lot of **3** much / a lot of / lots of **4** a lot of/ lots of

Much and many, some and any (Seite 24)
5a: many, some, a lot of, many, much, lots of, many, some, a lot of, any, lots of, lots of, many, any
5b: 1 any, anybody **2** something **3** anywhere, somewhere

Challenge
A very short history of communication (Seite 25)
1a: 1 Now computers... **2** In the stone age ... **3** People could buy ... **4** About 5,000 years ... **5** In the 20th ... **6** In 1876 ... **7** 600 years ago ...
1b: Individuelle Lösung

Checkout (Seite 26–27)
Speaking: Individuelle Lösung
Writing: Individuelle Lösung
Listening: 1 ~~10~~ – 20 **2** ~~cheese~~ – zucchini **3** ~~Italian~~ – vegan **4** ~~insects~~ – cheeses **5** ~~not~~ – definitely
Reading: 1 E **2** A **3** D **4** C
Mediation: 1 ~~keinen~~ – immer einen **2** ~~ihre eigene Kleidung~~ – Kleidung von der „Big Issue" **3** ~~kaufen~~ / ~~zum halben Preis~~ – bekommen / kostenlos **4** ~~£4~~ – £2
Grammar: 1 The chef was explaining how to make scrambled eggs from tofu. **2** Louis wasn't eating spicy insects. **3** We were talking about the "Big Issue". **4** My parents were asking about the school trip.
Vocabulary: 1 vegan – vegetarian **2** jobless – homeless **3** hopeless – hopeful **4** eat – post

Unit 3

Part A: Exploring the UK
Class trip reports (Seite 28)
1a: 1 wrong **2** wrong **3** not in the text **4** wrong **5** right **6** not in the text **7** wrong
1b: 1 Glasgow **2** train **3** almost 6 hours **4** to understand the guide **5** with a really strong accent **6** the highest mountain in the UK **7** haggis
1c: 1 St Austell **2** hostel **3** first half of the year **4** Mevagissey **5** Eden Project
My day in the UK (Seite 29)
2: Individuelle Lösung

A museum in Northern Ireland (Seite 29)
3: 1 J **2** O **3** U **4** R **5** N **6** E **7** Y

Comparing places (Seite 30)
4a: Individuelle Lösung
4b: 1 worse, worst **2** less, least **3** more, most

Part B: A class trip to Wales (Seite 31)
A trip to Wales
1: 1 3-4 **2** 8-10 **3** 16 **4** 21-24 **5** 31 **6** 34

At a hostel in Wales (Seite 31-32)
2a: Individuelle Lösung
2b: 7, 2, 6, 8, 4, 5, 1, 3
2c: 1 Menschen jeden Alters und jeder Nationalität **2** Die Lehrkräfte sind verantwortlich **3** Ein Bett/Zimmer wird nur bis zu dieser Zeit reserviert **4** Man kann anrufen oder beim Hostel fragen **5 a)** sie werden geteilt **b)** es gibt Familienzimmer **6 a)** sauber machen **b)** Tisch decken **7a)** Müll trennen **b)** Wasser und Energie sparen

My or mine? (Seite 33)
3: 1 my, Mine **2** theirs, Our **3** yours **4** Hers

How to move around in Wales (Seite 33)
4: 1 do, by – Ich mache eine Stadtrundfahrt mit dem Fahrrad. **2** ride – Die Schüler fahren mit dem Rad durch den Snowdonia National Park. **3** go, on – Sie fahren mit dem Bus zurück zum Hostel. **4** go skiing – Im Winter kann man auf dem Mount Snowdon Ski fahren.

Go, go, go! (Seite 33)
5: 1 go on **2** go ahead **3** go online **4** going crazy **5** go without **6** go for
In German: **1** Nicht aufhören, wir müssen weiter. Es wird dunkel. **2** Jetzt bist du dran. Mach weiter. **3** Unser Wifi funktioniert nicht. Ich kann nicht online gehen. **4** Es ist so viel Arbeit! Ich werde wirklich verrückt. **5** Ich habe nicht genug Geld für eine weitere Reise. Ich muss darauf verzichten. **6** Komm schon, lauf schneller! Hol dir Gold!

Part C: Visiting Birmingham
Birmingham (Seite 34)
1a: 1 Bull Ring shopping centre **2** Victoria Square **3** The Canals **4** Bournville Chocolate Factory **5** Birmingham Town Hall
1b: 2, 5, 3, 4, 1

At a café in Birmingham (Seite 34)
2: 2 know what Groaty pudding is. **4** ein Gericht wie Haferbrei mit Rindfleisch **6** Are there other dishes typical to the area? **8** Sie haben Balti Curry – die britische Version wurde 1970 in Birmingham erfunden. **10** That sounds good. We'll have three curries please.

At a car boot sale (Seite 35)
3a: book, sunglasses, scarf
3b: Book – 2, Sunglasses – 12, Scarf – 3.50
3c: 1 sale **2** sell **3** buy **4** change **5** customer **6** expensive

A car boot sale story (Seite 35)
4: Individuelle Lösung

Different times (Seite 36)
5a: *simple present:* often, every day, always, on Mondays, sometimes. *present progressive:* at the moment, right now, this week. *simple past:* last year, a week ago, yesterday. *present perfect:* lately, already, just, up to now, ever, not ... yet
5b: 1 at the moment – Amy and Ben are walking around the car boot sale at the moment. **2** just – Ben has just bought a T-shirt. **3** often – Amy and Ben often spend time together.
5c: 1 Ben war noch nie auf einem Flohmarkt. **2** Ben hat gerade seine Klassenfahrt beendet. **3** Ben ist jetzt seit zwei Tagen in Birmingham. The tenses are the same in English but change in German.

Challenge
Working with words (Seite 37)
1a, 1b, 1c: Individuelle Lösung

Checkout (Seite 38–39)
Speaking: Individuelle Lösung
Writing: Individuelle Lösung
Reading: 1 train **2** 1.5 hours **3** sweets **4** learned how to make chocolate
Listening: 1 wrong **2** right **3** wrong **4** wrong **5** right
Mediation: 1 in Edinburgh, Schottland **2** im Jahr 1955 **3** altes Spielzeug, Spiele, Klamotten und Bücher **4** eine Puppe von 1740
Grammar: a) 1 Alice has eaten breakfast on the train. **2** They have seen colourful houseboats. **3** We have visited an open-air museum.
b) 1 mine **2** his **3** ours **4** yours / hers
Vocabulary: 1 museum – not a place to stay
2 coach – not a type of food
3 journey – not a means of transport

Unit 4

Part A: Welcome to Scotland
A video chat (Seite 40)
1: 1 traditional **2** two handles **3** too English **4** Scotland **5** a bagpipe player live **6** to his favourite restaurant **7** haggis for a long time **8** to the Highlands **9** are beautiful

Dad in Scotland (Seite 40)
2: 1 husband **2** kilts **3** juice **4** dance floor **5** bagpipe **6** castle **7** long **8** pictures

What they have done (Seite 41)
3: ... drunk juice. Andrew has worn a kilt before and he has visited Edinburgh castle. Jack hasn't played the bagpipes before, but he has played the guitar. Philip has danced all night long before, but he hasn't been as happy as he is now with Andrew.

A conversation (Seite 41–42)
4a: They are talking about tomorrow in Edinburgh
4b: Have: 1, 2, 3, 5 Have not: 4, 6
4c: She has walked down the Royal Mile. She has eaten haggis. She has not gone on a tour around Edinburgh. She has visited the National Museum of Scotland. She has not bought something at the market.

Working with words (Seite 42)
5a: drums – instrument
quaich – cup, handles
kilt – clothing, a Scottish skirt with a pattern
beach – landscape, There is lots of sand and the sea.
5b: Individuelle Lösung

Part B: A trip to Edinburgh
Welcome to Edinburgh (Seite 43)
1a: 1 wrong **2** wrong **3** right **4** right **5** wrong **6** right **7** wrong
1b: 1 D **2** A **3** F **4** E **5** B
1c: Individuelle Lösung

What do you need for Scottish porridge? (Seite 43)
2: 1 1 pinch of salt **2** 280 ml milk **3** 115 g oats **4** 1 tbsp berries or jam **5** 2-3 tbsp maple syrup or brown sugar

A song (Seite 44)
3: 1 Have you ever been to London? **2** Have you ever met a T. rex? **3** Have you ever eaten snake? **4** Have you ever done a backflip? **5** Have you ever done a marathon?

Lots of questions (Seite 44–45)
4a: 1 been **2** met **3** visited **4** cooked **5** eaten **6** forgotten
4b: Individuelle Lösung

Lots of questions (Seite 45)
5a: 1 potatoes **2** milk **3** eggs **4** turnips **5** jam **6** chocolate bar
5b: Individuelle Lösung

Part C: Loch Ness
A second trip to Loch Ness (Seite 46)
1a: 1 Tia and Jack went back to Loch Ness.
2 They looked for the monster in the lake.
3 They saw something strange in the lake.
1b: Individuelle Lösung
1c: Individuelle Lösung

Did you know? (Seite 47)
2a: lakes, kilometres, wonderful
2b: 1 It is the only island on the lake and is man-made. **2** Dead plants make the water very dark **3** They want to try and spot the monster.

A boat tour (Seite 47)
3: 1 Die Touren finden zwischen 10 Uhr und

18 Uhr statt. Im Sommer gibt es eine Tour um 20 Uhr. **2** Leute, denen schnell kalt wird **3** Am Tag der Tour oder online im Voraus. **4** Auf der Rückseite des Flyers **5** Für den Fall, dass man Nessie sieht!

Hello from Scotland (Seite 48)
4: 1 come **2** tried **3** been **4** walked
5 been **6** bought

Tourists at Loch Ness (Seite 48)
5: 1 However **2** After **3** before **4** so **5** Before
6 but

Challenge
A travel blog (Seite 49)
1a: 1 Hi everyone!... **2** We took the train... **3** After the hotel... **4** After Edinburgh castle... **5** Because it was raining... **6** We were really full... **7** Then we got...
1b: Individuelle Lösung
1c: Individuelle Lösung

Check out (Seite 50–51)
Speaking: Individuelle Lösung
Writing: Individuelle Lösung
Listening: 1 Scotland **2** Edinburgh **3** about five hours **4** Aberdeen **5** around 1 p.m. **6** have lunch
Mediation: 1 Die Straße ist unterirdisch (und sehr eng). **2** Straßen wurden oft nach wichtigen Menschen benannt. **3** Mary King war eine erfolgreiche Geschäftsfrau.
Reading: 1 wrong **2** wrong **3** right **4** wrong **5** not in the text **6** right
Grammar: 1 Gemma has already played the bagpipes. **2** Charlie has recently been to a ceilidh. **3** Sue and Gordon have cooked haggis for their family. **4** Mara has already finished her homework.
Vocabulary: 1 wedding **2** lakes **3** tattie **4** century **5** book **6** Lad

Unit 5

Part A: The United States of America
Preparing for the United States (Seite 52)
1: 1 alle drei **2** in the east and west **3** its beaches, creative people **4** lots of space, a big river **5** sun on earth

Stamford climate (Seite 52)
2: 1 wrong **2** not in the text **3** right **4** wrong **5** wrong **6** right **7** not in the text

Jack's host family replies (Seite 53)
3: 1 will be a wonderful experience **2** will help with the household tasks **3** will show you around **4** will be a great way to make new friends **5** will see you at the airport

Will or won't? (Seite 53)
4: 1 will live **2** will make **3** won't know **4** will be
5 won't get **6** won't forget

A weather song (Seite 54)
5: Individuelle Lösung

Weather on another planet (Seite 54)
6: Individuelle Lösung

Part B: Small town life
Jack's email (Seite 55)
1a: 1 A special training **2** Jack's host family
3 How to protect the environment **4** Introducing Stamford **5** A great trip
1b: 1 host family - not to do with protecting the environment **2** compost - not something you eat **3** tornado - not somewhere you live **4** shopping mall - not to do with safety

Writing an email (Seite 55)
2a: 1 1 **2** 2–6 **3** 7–23 **4** 24–27 **5** 28–30 **6** 31
2b: Individuelle Lösung
2c: Individuelle Lösung

British or American? (Seite 56)
3a: 1 farm – American **2** sister – British **3** exciting – British **4** rainwater – American **5** host – British **6** tornadoes – American **7** Tuesday – American **8** Tube – British
3b: Individuelle Lösung

What will happen to the polar bears? (Seite 57)
4: 1 will you be **2** How will you start **3** What will happen **4** Will they disappear **5** What will you say **6** What effect will it have **7** How will they do **8** Will you present

Storm hunters (Seite 57)
5: Storm hunters suchen extreme Wettersituationen, oft Stürme, um mehr über sie herauszufinden. Sie sehen sich häufig Tornados in verschiedenen Größen an.

Part C: New York City
In New York City (Seite 58)
1a: 1 water - air conditioning **2** motorbike riders – cyclists **3** an urban – a solar panel **4** the zoo of the park – The High Line **5** animals – new techniques for growing food
1b: 1 1 hour **2** 4/N **3** 35 minutes **4** Ellis, Governors

Tour of a green roof (Seite 58)
2: 1 Yes, there are more birds and insects because of the green roof. **2** The solar panels can't power the Javits Center on their own. **3** They don't know how much exactly. But the Center uses less energy than before. **4** Yes, but a green roof needs a lot of planning and money.

The Statue of Liberty (Seite 59)
3: 1 ~~fünf~~ – drei **2** ~~die Krone der Freiheitsstatue~~ – nur die Museen **3** ~~muss extra gebucht werden~~ – ist im Ticket drin **4** ~~die Freiheitsstatue~~ – den Sicherheitsbereich

My visit to the Statue of Liberty (Seite 59)
4: Individuelle Lösung

A sustainable city (Seite 60)
5: 1 environment **2** solar panels **3** renewable **4** sustainability **5** wildlife **6** urban

Our future (Seite 60)
6: Individuelle Lösung

Challenge
More practice: guided writing (Seite 61)
1a: Individuelle Lösung
1b: Individuelle Lösung

Check out (Seite 50–51)
Speaking: Individuelle Lösung
Writing: Individuelle Lösung
Listening: 1 Amy **2** A point system for vegan and vegetarian food in the cafeteria. **3** It's a really good idea. **4** a vegan chocolate bar **5** talk to a teacher about the idea
Mediation: 1 ein Monatsabo **2** 10.000 Fahrräder **3** gar nichts / es ist kostenlos **4** $19 pro Tag **5** 1000 Stationen
Reading: 1 go to an after-school club **2** Theater Club **3** meet my friends after school or after the clubs **4** go to the movies or just hang out at the mall **5** Do you have clubs at your school? And if yes, do you have a favorite? / What do you do after school?
Grammar: a) 1 The school bus leaves at 7 a.m. **2** I think you will like the food there. **3** We are visiting my grandma tomorrow. **4** Oliver and his friends are going to the movies after school tomorrow. **5** The concert starts at 6 p.m. **6** It will be so much fun! **7** The friends are meeting this afternoon. **8** My mum thinks it will be too cold to meet outside.
b) predictions / instant decisions I think you will like the food there. / It will be so much fun! / My mum thinks it will be too cold to meet outside.

scheduled events The school bus leaves at 7 a.m. / The concert starts at 6 p.m.
plans We are visiting my grandma tomorrow. / Oliver and his friends are going to the movies after school tomorrow. / The friends are meeting this afternoon.
Vocabulary: 1 chips **2** cinema **3** sneakers **4** holiday

Unit 6

Part A: US school life

A typical day at school (Seite 64)
1: 1 Jack wants to tell people about his school day in the USA. **2** On the school bus, Jack does his homework or talks to his friends. **3** When he gets to school, Jack puts his lunch and books in his locker. **4** Jack's schedule is easy to remember because he has the same subjects every day. **5** On Friday, Jack is going to support the school basketball team. **6** Jack's friends are going to make him jealous because they are going on a school trip without him.

Join the club (Seite 64)
2: 1 falsch **2** richtig **3** nicht im Text **4** richtig **5** nicht im Text **6** richtig **7** falsch **8** nicht im Text

Morning announcements (Seite 65)
3a: 1 eco club meeting **2** holiday bake sale **3** yearbook meeting **4** swim team **5** chess tournament **6** Seaside Center trip
3b: 1 at lunch **2** $2 **3** next week **4** the girls' team **5** everyone **6** room 104

Odd one out (Seite 65)
4: 1 school bus – board **2** school spirit – restroom **3** announcements – science **4** restroom – swim club **5** locker – subject **6** bus ride – German

A school crossword (Seite 66)
5: Across 2 period **4** geography **5** schedule **8** favorite **Down 1** library **3** hall pass **6** chorus **7** math

Plans for the green club (Seite 66)
6: 1 The club is going to give away seeds for home gardens. **2** The club isn't going to spend any money on advertising. **3** The club is going to look for more guest speakers. **4** The club isn't going to ignore new students' ideas. **5** They are going to serve more vegetables in the school cafeteria. **6** They are not going to organize workshops the day before a holiday.

Part B: At the *Super Bowl*

A super event (Seite 67)
1: 1 lines 6 and 7 **2** line 10 **3** line 15 **4** line 18 **5** lines 23-26 **6** lines 23, 24 and 27

After the game (Seite 67)
2: Individuelle Lösung

A phone call with a friend (Seite 68)
3a: the atmosphere at the game, the half-time show, the celebration after the game, plans to meet
3b: 1 wrong **2** right **3** right **4** wrong **5** right **6** wrong **7** right **8** right

Stadium rules (Seite 68–69)
4a: 3, 5, 1, 6, 2, 4
4b: 1 am Eingang / bei der Ticketkontrolle **2** Essen und Getränke, große Taschen und Feuerwerk **3** in den richtigen Mülleimer werfen **4** die Ansagen beachten und die Anweisungen der Mitarbeitenden befolgen
4c: Individuelle Lösung

Questions (Seite 69)
5: 1 Who is going to buy tickets for the game? **2** Is your girlfriend going to come with us?

3 What snacks are you going to take? **4** Why aren't your parents going to drive you to the stadium? **5** Am I going to need money for souvenirs?

Part C: Travelling the USA
A trip to the west coast (Seite 70)
1a: Green travel and green projects
1b: 1 reusable **2** solar panels **3** Electric **4** sustainable **5** renewable **6** forests / rainforests and oceans **7** natural

Similar word, different meaning (Seite 70)
2a: 1 root: help, suffixes: –ful, –less **2** root: new, prefix: re– **3** root: sustainable, prefix: un–
2b: The prefix *re–* means you do something again (here: make something new again). The prefix *un–* makes the word negative (here: not sustainable). The suffix *–ful* means there is a lot of something (here: a lot of help). The suffix *–less* means you don't have something (here: no help).
Hinweis: The suffix *–able* means something is possible or you are able to do something (here: it is possible to sustain (the environment) with the thing that is sustainable).
2c: Individuelle Lösung

National parks in the USA (Seite 71)
3: Warum Nationalparks wichtig sind: Sie schützen lokale Tiere und Pflanzen. **Erster Nationalpark in den USA:** Yellowstone National Park **Standort des ältesten Baums:** White Mountains, California **Genaue Position des ältesten Baums ist geheim, weil:** er geschützt werden soll **Höhe des Mount Denali in Alaska:** 6.168 m hoch

A big country (Seite 71)
4: Portland to Philadelphia: 2864 miles, 4609 km, 42 hours **Los Angeles to San Diego:** 120 miles, 193 km, 2 hours **Miami to Minneapolis:** 1795 miles, 2888 km, 26 hours
Getting around Bavaria (Seite 71)
5: Individuelle Lösung

Whale watching (Seite 72)
6: are going to leave, see, was, is getting, will see, were sailing, got, was, have learned, have identified, is, are going to start, will help, is giving

Challenge
More practice: listening (Seite 73)
1a: 1 in a coffee shop **2** at the park **3** in the kitchen **4** at the shopping mall **5** in a restaurant
1b: 1 B – The Eagles **2** B – guessing who will win **3** C – it' making the fans angry at other fans **4** A – scared **5** C – famous singers perform
1c: 1 by bus from the airport (1 detail), by car (1 detail), by ferry (1 detail) **2** 24 hours a day **3** $30 **4** $55

Check out (Seite 74–75)
Speaking: Individuelle Lösung
Writing: Individuelle Lösung
Reading: 1 line 2 **2** lines 3 and 4 **3** lines 5 and 6 **4** lines 6 and 7 **5** line 10 **6** line 11
Mediation: Wann erfunden: im späten neunzehnten Jahrhundert
Anzahl der Spieler pro Team: 11 Spieler
Wie werden Punkte erzeilt? Der Fußball muss hinter der Ziellinie des anderen Teams sein.
Wer gewinnt? Das Team mit den meisten Punkten am Ende des Spiels.
Typische Dauer eines Spiels: ca. 3 Stunden
Kosten für Werbung während des Super Bowl: $7 Millionen für 30 Sekunden
Listening: 1 ~~every day~~ – on Mondays, Wednesdays and Fridays **2** ~~French~~ – app development **3** ~~morning~~ – afternoon OR ~~Spanish~~ – art, PE and German **4** ~~Tuesdays~~ – Fridays
Grammar: a) 1 Mr Turner is going to watch the Super Bowl. **2** Robin is going to bake cookies.

3 Terry and Sally are going to go hiking.
b) 1 Is Mr Turner going to watch the Super Bowl?
2 Is Robin going to bake cookies?
3 What are Terry and Sally going to do?
Vocabulary: 1 homerooom **2** cap / gown
3 lockers **4** elective **5** states **6** hurricane

A trip to Wales

1 skill: reading TB p. 164

Read the text on page 58 in your textbook again. In which line(s) can you find …

1 … that Ben is not happy? line(s): ______

2 … why they took the bus? line(s): ______

3 … what "reception" means in Welsh? line(s): ______

4 … that the children can't decide which sandcastle is the best? line(s): ______

5 … what Ben actually sees from the top of the mountain? line(s): ______

6 … that the children can decide what they want to do on their last day? line(s): ______

At a hostel in Wales

2a skill: writing TB p. 165

You would like to stay in a Welsh hostel. Write an email with information and questions. Write about:

1 when you are coming and how long you are staying
2 with how many people you are coming
3 if there are free rooms and how much they cost
4 one more question you have

New Message

Dear Gwen,

2b

In the hostel you find an information board. What do the symbols mean? Match the signs and their meanings.

☐ 
☐ 

☐ 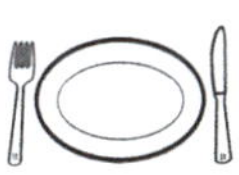
☐ 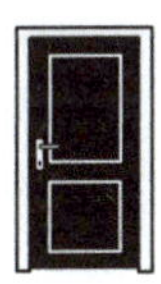
☐ 
☐ 
☐ 
☐ 

1 Wi-Fi
2 clothes washing facilities
3 bedding provided
4 showers
5 fully heated
6 dining room
7 waste disposal area
8 private rooms available

2c skill: mediation TB p. 166

Auch auf der Webseite des Hostels gibt es einige Informationen. Schaue sie dir an und bearbeite die Aufgaben (1–6) stichpunktartig auf Deutsch. Ein Wort genügt nicht.

Youth Hostel Rules

The Welsh Youth Hostel Association (YHA) hopes that a stay in our houses is a great experience for all our guests who are of different ages and countries. That's why we have rules that help all our guests to have a fantastic time. Group leaders and teachers are responsible for their groups.

Arrival

- Visitors with reservations can arrange their arrival time individually with the hostel management.
- Booked beds will be kept for you until 6 p.m., then they may be given to other visitors.
- Visitors without reservations can call or ask in the youth hostel to find out if there is a free room. If you want a guaranteed room, please book online in advance.

Staying in a Youth Hostel

- The guests are accommodated in shared bedrooms and usually separated by gender.
- Families can get a family room if it is available.
- The YHA depends on a helping hand from our visitors. We need your assistance with jobs such as
  - cleaning and tidying up the equipment, rooms and items you have used during your stay
  - setting and clearing tables

The youth hostels help to protect our nature. Visitors are therefore requested to collect waste separately, avoid waste, avoid plastic, and to be economical in their use of electricity, heating and water.

1 Welche Gäste übernachten in den Hostels?

______

2 Wer trägt die Verantwortung bei Schulklassen?

______

3 Was muss man beachten, wenn man nach 18 Uhr anreist?

______

4 Was kann man machen, wenn man vorab kein Zimmer reserviert hat?

______

5 Nenne zwei wichtige Informationen zu den Zimmern.

a) ______ b) ______

6 Wie müssen Gäste das Team des Hostels unterstützen? Nenne zwei Aufgaben.

a) ______ b) ______

7 Wie kann man als Gast die Umwelt schützen? Nenne zwei Aspekte.

a) ______ b) ______

My or mine?

3

Fill in the gaps. Choose the correct word from the brackets.

1 This isn't ______________ **(my / mine)** sandcastle. ______________ **(My / Mine)** was bigger!

2 Oh, look at ______________ **(their / theirs)**. ______________ **(Our / Ours)** sandcastles need more shells.

3 I've got lots of photos with my friends. Should I take some of you with ______________ **(your / yours)**?

4 I like Tia's sandcastle more than Declan's. ______________ **(Her/Hers)** has got more towers than his.

How to move around in Wales

4

Circle the right word. Then write down the German version.

1 I **do / make** a sightseeing tour **with the / by** bike.

____

____

2 The students **ride / drive** their bikes through Snowdonia National Park.

____

____

3 They **go / drive** back to the hostel **on / in** the bus.

____

____

4 In winter you can **go skiing / drive ski** on Mount Snowdon.

____

____

Go, go, go!

5

***Go* + *xx* can have different meanings. Fill in the gaps with the right words from the box. Use the right form of *go*. Then talk to a partner: How would you express the different meanings of *go* + *xx* in German?**

go online · go crazy · go on · go without · go for · go ahead

1 Don't stop, we must ______________. It's getting dark.

2 It's your turn. ______________.

3 Our Wi-Fi doesn't work. I can't ______________.

4 It's so much work! I'm really ______________!

5 I don't have enough money for another trip. I have to ______________.

6 Come on, run faster! ______________ gold!

Birmingham

1a skill: reading TB p. 164

Read the text on page 62 in your textbook again. Then write down what the pictures show.

1 

2 

3 

4 

5 

1b

Put the pictures from 1a in the right order as mentioned in the text. Then tell a partner about Ben and Amy's tour. Use the words *second, then, first, finally, next*.

At a café in Birmingham

2 skill: mediation TB p. 166

You are in a café in Birmingham. There is also a German family who doesn't speak much English. Help them talk to the waiter. Fill in the speech bubbles in German and English. Don't translate every single word.

German family	you	waiter
1 Was ist denn ein Groaty Pudding?	2 *They would like to* ______	3 It's a porridge-like meal with beef. Very good.
	4 *Groaty Pudding ist* ______	
5 Das hört sich interessant an. Gibt es auch andere landestypische Gerichte?	6 ______	7 We serve a fantastic Balti curry. It's originally from Northern India but the British version was invented in Birmingham in the 1970s.
	8 ______	
9 Klingt gut. Das nehmen wir. Dreimal bitte.	10 ______	11 I understood that. Good choice.

At a car boot sale

3a audio 1/37, skill: listening TB p. 163

Listen to the three dialogues at a car boot sale. What do the customers buy?

a scarf · a pair of shoes · a book · earrings · sunglasses · a football

You can say:
The girl buys ...

3b audio 1/37

Listen again. How much do the customers pay in the end? Complete the table.

thing			
price (£)			

3c

What are the car boot sale words? Write them down.

1 seɪl ______

2 sel ______

3 baɪ ______

4 tʃeɪndʒ ______

5 ˈkʌstəmə ______

6 ɪkˈspensɪv ______

A car boot sale story

4 skill: writing TB p. 165

Write a story about Ben and Amy at the car boot sale. Choose a title from the box. Write about 60 words.

At the car boot sale · Great deal! · Great things to buy · Just junk · What a bargain! · Oh, what a day!

Title: ______

Different times

5a

Complete the table with the signal words from the box.

at the moment · lately · often · ~~today~~ · last year · ~~usually~~ · every day · already · right now · just · up to now · always · ever · this week · a week ago · not ... yet · on Mondays · sometimes · yesterday

simple present	present progressive	simple past	present perfect
usually	*today*		

5b

Underline the signal words. Then write sentences. Pay attention to the right tense and word order.

0 Ben – yesterday – take – a lot of photos

Ben took a lot of photos yesterday.

1 Amy and Ben – at the moment – walk – around – car boot sale

2 Ben – just – buy – T-shirt

3 Amy and Ben – often – spend – together – time

5c

Write the sentences in German.
What is the difference between the tenses in English and in German? Talk to a partner.

1 Ben has never been to a car boot sale. ______

2 Ben has just finished his class trip. ______

3 Ben has been in Birmingham for two days now. ______

Working with words

1a skill: working with words TB p. 162

Choose a topic and make a word web about it. Here are some ideas. You can draw more boxes in the word web.

holidays · travelling · the London Tube · food · social media · a car boot sale · ...

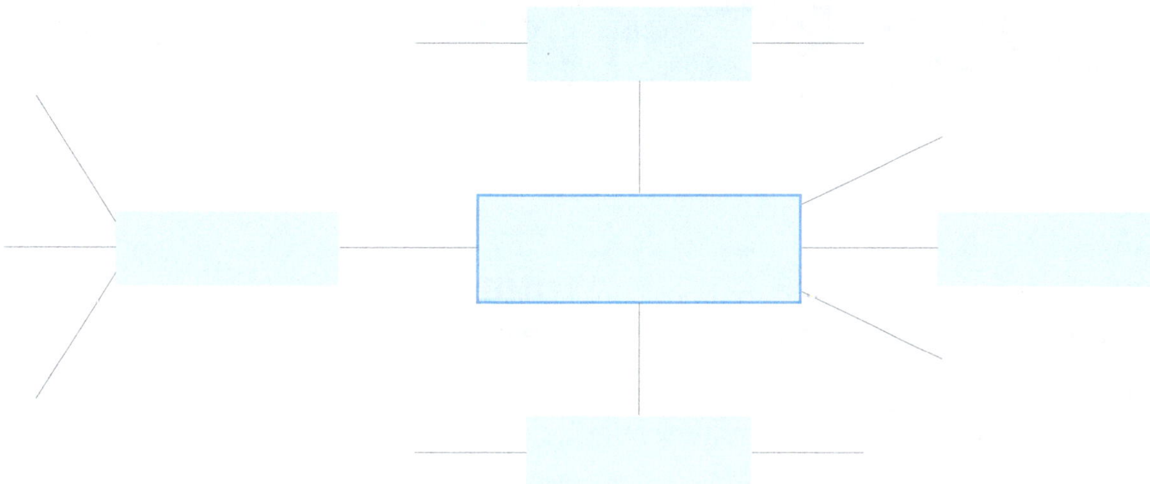

1b

Choose four words from your word web in 1a and write down the opposite, a synonym or another word that usually goes with it.

0 *spend ↔ save* OR *spend = give* OR *spend money, spend time*

1 ______

2 ______

3 ______

4 ______

1c

Are there any words in your word web that you find difficult? Write them down. Then draw a picture about the word, use it in a sentence or try to explain it with other words.

1 ______

2 ______

Check out

Speaking solutions p. 78

Look at the pictures. Use the adjectives in the box to compare them. Talk to a partner.

far · high · old · big / small · interesting · new · popular · cheap / expensive · nice

Big Ben

Stonehenge

hotel

hostel

fish and chips

pizza

I can: compare things. ◯

Reading solutions p. 78

Read the report and circle the correct answers.

Last week we went to Birmingham. Our train left at 7.15 a.m. and we arrived at 8.45 a.m. We had "breakfast" (lots of sweets) on the train, which was really nice. In Birmingham, we first took a walk along the canals. There were so many colourful house-boats! Then, we looked at Birmingham Town Hall and the Library of Birmingham. The library is a funny building. It looks a bit like a toy. In the afternoon, we visited Cadbury World where we learned about how chocolate is made. We also bought a lot of chocolate for our train journey home. *Alice Jones, class 8LB*

0 Class 8LB went to: Belfast | Glasgow | Birmingham.
1 They went there by: bus | train | plane.
2 The journey there took: 1.5 hours | 2 hours | 3 hours.
3 On the train they ate apples | sweets | chips.
4 They visited the Cadbury chocolate factory and: ate a lot of chocolate | learned how to make chocolate | talked a lot about chocolate.

I can: understand a report about a trip. ◯

Writing solutions p. 78

You went to a car boot sale in your holidays. Write a diary entry about it. Write about 60 words and include the following:

- where the car boot sale was
- what you bought and what it cost
- how you liked it there

Use your exercise book.

I can: write about holiday experiences. ◯

Listening audio 1/41, solutions p. 78

Listen. Are the statements right or wrong?

	✓	✗
1 The class met at Heathrow Airport.		
2 They went to Wales.		
3 They went to a very boring museum.		
4 It was a museum about ships.		
5 They also took a walk around the city.		

I can: understand a message about a class trip. ◯

Mediation solutions p. 78

Lies das Schild. Beantworte die Fragen stichpunktartig auf Deutsch. Ein Wort genügt nicht.

Museum of Childhood
At the Museum of Childhood you can learn about how children grew up in the past. You can look at old toys, games, clothes, and books. The oldest toy we have is a doll from 1740. There are also many items from 1900 to 2000. Come with your parents and grandparents and see what they played with when they were little. The museum opened in 1955, and it is the first museum of its kind in the world.
Entry: free
Opening times: every day from 10 a.m. to 5 p.m.
Address: 42 High Street, Royal Mile, Edinburgh, EH1 1TG

1 Wo ist das Museum? ______

2 Wann wurde das Museum eröffnet? ______

3 Was kann man noch dort ansehen? ______

4 Was ist das älteste Spielzeug dort und von wann ist es? ______

I can: understand important information on a sign. ○

USE OF ENGLISH

Grammar solutions p. 78

a) What have they done on their trip? Write sentences. Use the *present perfect*.

0 Class 8LB (be) to Birmingham. *Class 8LB has been to Birmingham.*

1 Alice (eat) breakfast on the train. ______

2 They (see) colourful houseboats. ______

3 We (visit) an open-air museum. ______

b) Write the correct *possessive pronouns* for the blue words.

1 Is this your book or **my book**? ______

2 I have looked at her photos but not at **his photos**. ______

3 Is their teacher as nice as **our teacher**? ______

4 Are these notes **your notes** or **her notes**? ______ ______

Vocabulary solutions p. 78

Circle the odd word out and explain your choice.

0 kayaking | talking | hiking | paddleboarding *"Talking" is not a sport*

1 hotel | youth hostel | museum | guesthouse ______

2 haggis | chocolate | fish and chips | coach ______

3 journey | coach | train | plane ______

I can: write about things that link past and present, and use pronouns. ○

use vocabulary to describe regions in the UK. ○

A video chat

1

Read the text on page 74 in your textbook again. Complete the sentences with information from the text.

0 Ben hasn't been to a wedding yet .

1 Jack said that his uncle's wedding was quite ______ .

2 A 'quaich' is a cup with ______ .

3 Tia and Jack's dad didn't wear a kilt because he has become ______ .

4 Jack wasn't born in ______ .

5 Emma has never heard ______ .

6 Tomorrow Uncle Andrew is taking Tia and Jack ______ .

7 Tia and Jack's dad hasn't eaten ______ .

8 On Tuesday, Tia and Jack are going ______ .

9 Declan has heard that the Highlands ______ .

Dad in Scotland

2

Read what Tia and Jack's dad says about Scotland. Fill in the right words.

Yesterday, we went to my brother's wedding ('wedɪŋ). We all had a great time! My brother looked so happy with his ______ (↔ **wife**) Philip and they both looked fantastic in their traditional ______ ().Everyone drank from a quaich. We drank whisky from it, but the kids had ______ (dʒu:s). My wife usually hates dancing, but she has never had as much fun on the ______ () as last night! Oh, and there was even a ______ ('bægpaɪp) player! Tomorrow we are going to Edinburgh. Jack is really excited about the ______ (). I haven't eaten haggis for a ______ (↔ **short**) time so I can't wait to eat it again! I am definitely going to take a lot of ______ ('pɪktʃəz).

What they have done

3 grammar in short: 11 present perfect

Write about what the people have and haven't done before.

Tia
✗ drink from a quaich
✓ drink juice

Jack
✗ play the bagpipes
✓ play the guitar

Uncle Andrew
✓ wear a kilt
✓ visit Edinburgh castle

Philip
✓ dance all night long
✗ be as happy as he is now with Andrew

Tia hasn't drunk from a quaich before, but she has …

A conversation

4a audio 2/4

Listen to Tia and Jack's parents. Which sentence summarises what they are talking about best? Tick (✓).

- ☐ They are talking about their holiday next year.
- ☐ They are talking about tomorrow in Edinburgh.
- ☐ They are talking about their time at Andrew and Philip's wedding.

4b audio 2/4

Listen again. What has Tia and Jack's mum done in Edinburgh before (✓)? What hasn't she done (✗)?

1 visit Edinburgh Castle ☐
2 walk down the Royal Mile ☐
3 eat haggis ☐
4 go on a tour around Edinburgh ☐
5 visit the National Museum of Scotland ☐
6 buy something at a market ☐

4c

Write down sentences using the information in 4b.

Tia and Jack's mum has visited Edinburgh Castle. She has ...

Working with words

5a

Complete the table with umbrella terms from the box and your own explanations. There are more umbrella terms in the box than you need.

animal · clothing · cup · food · hobby · instrument · landscape

word	umbrella term	explanation
juice	It's a type of drink.	It is cold with fruit and you often have it at breakfast.
drums	It's a type of ____________.	They are very loud and you hit them with sticks.
quaich	It's a type of ____________.	It is Scottish and has two ____________.
kilt	It's a type of ____________.	It is ____________.
beach	It's a type of ____________.	____________.

5b

Choose two more words from the word list on textbook pages 197–199 and fill in the table. Read out the umbrella term and explanation to a partner. Your partner has to guess what the word is.

word	umbrella term	explanation

1 DIE EINFACHE VERGANGENHEIT: AUSSAGEN (REVISION)

the simple past: statements TB p. 144

Wenn du über etwas sprechen willst, das in der Vergangenheit liegt und abgeschlossen ist, verwendest du die einfache Vergangenheit *(simple past)*. Bei regelmäßigen Verben bildest du es, indem du die Endung *-ed* an die Grundform anhängst. Die Formen der unregelmäßigen Verben musst du lernen.

They had bad weather.
We went to the beach.

It was really relaxing.
We were in Wales.

Die Verneinung im *simple past* bildest du bei allen Personen mit *didn't* (= *did not*). Danach kommt dann das Verb in der Grundform. Bei *was* und *were* hängst du *not* oder die Kurzform *n't* an, wenn du einen verneinten Satz bilden willst.

We didn't visit our family.
Declan didn't hear his alarm.

It wasn't great fun.
The children weren't on holiday.

2 DIE EINFACHE VERGANGENHEIT: FRAGEN (REVISION)

the simple past: questions TB p. 145

Bei Entscheidungsfragen im *simple past* stellst du *did* an den Satzanfang. *Did* ist bei allen Personen gleich. Danach folgt das Verb in der Grundform. In der Kurzantwort wird *did* wieder aufgegriffen.

Did you go abroad?	Yes, we did.	No, we didn't.
Did Declan stay at home?	Yes, he did.	No, he didn't.

Bei Fragen mit *was* und *were* brauchst du kein *did*. Hier steht *was* oder *were* am Satzanfang. In der Kurzantwort wird *was* oder *were* wieder aufgegriffen: Was the weather good? Yes, it was./No, it wasn't.

Bei Fragen mit Fragewort steht das Fragewort am Satzanfang: **What** did you do in the holidays? **Where** did she stay?

Wenn *who* nach dem Subjekt fragt, brauchst du kein zusätzliches *did*: **Who** went abroad?

Auch bei Fragen mit *was* und *were* brauchst du kein *did*: **How** was the tour? **What** were the activities like?

Dustys Hinweis

Du findest eine Liste mit unregelmäßigen Verben in deinem Buch ab S. 258.

Diese Formen musst du wie Vokabeln lernen.

3 DIE VERLAUFSFORM DER GEGENWART: AUSSAGEN (REVISION)

present progressive: statements TB p. 146

Wenn du ausdrücken möchtest, dass jemand etwas jetzt gerade tut oder dass etwas in diesem Moment stattfindet, kannst du das mit dem *present progressive* tun. Du bildest es mit einer Form von *be* sowie der Grundform des Verbs *+ing*. Signalwörter für die Verwendung des *present progressive* sind zum Beispiel *at the moment, (right) now, today* und *this week*.

I am finishing my maths homework.
You are eating.

Her friend is talking on the phone.
Her brothers are playing in the garden.

Für die Verneinung fügst du *not* hinter der Form von *be* ein. Hier wird dann häufig die Kurzform verwendet.

I am not writing a text. → I'm not writing a text.
She is not shopping. → She isn't shopping.
They are not eating. → They aren't eating.

4 DIE VERLAUFSFORM DER GEGENWART: FRAGEN (REVISION)

present progressive: questions TB p. 147

Mit dem *present progressive* kannst du fragen, was jemand gerade tut. Bei Entscheidungsfragen stellst du eine Form von *be* an den Satzanfang. Man antwortet darauf meist mit einer Kurzantwort.

Am I dreaming?	Yes, you are.	No, you aren't.
Are you doing your homework?	Yes, I am.	No, I'm not.
Are they dancing?	Yes, they are.	No, they aren't.

Bei Fragen mit Fragewort steht das Fragewort am Satzanfang.

What are you doing?
Where is Pete going?

5 DIE BEFEHLSFORM (REVISION)

the imperative TB p. 148

So kannst du jemanden um etwas bitten oder auffordern, etwas zu tun (Befehlsform):

Wait a minute!
Keep walking along the road.

Wenn jemand etwas *nicht* tun soll, kannst du das so sagen (verneinte Befehlsform):

Don't make it so complicated!
Don't turn into that street.

6 DIE VERLAUFSFORM DER VERGANGENHEIT: AUSSAGEN

past progressive: statements TB p. 149

Wenn du ausdrücken möchtest, was zu einem bestimmten Zeitpunkt in der Vergangenheit gerade passierte, kannst du das mit dem *past progressive* tun. Das *past progressive* wird ganz ähnlich gebildet wie das *present progressive*, nur dass die Form von *be* im *simple past* steht.

I was finishing my maths homework.
You were eating.

Her friend was talking on the phone.
Her brothers were playing in the garden.

Für die Verneinung fügst du *not* hinter der Form von *be* ein. Hier wird dann häufig die Kurzform verwendet.

She was not shopping. → She wasn't shopping.
They were not eating. → They weren't eating.

7 DIE VERLAUFSFORM DER VERGANGENHEIT: FRAGEN

past progressive: questions TB p. 150

Entscheidungsfragen im *past progressive* bildest du, indem du *was / were* an den Satzanfang stellst. In der Kurzantwort wird *was / were* aufgegriffen.

Was I dreaming?	Yes, you were.	No, you weren't.
Were you doing your homework?	Yes, I was.	No, I wasn't.
Were they dancing?	Yes, they were.	No, they weren't.

Bei Fragen mit Fragewort steht das Fragewort am Satzanfang.

What were you doing?
Where was Pete going?

Dustys Hinweis

Wenn du beschreiben möchtest, was in der Vergangenheit gerade vor sich ging, als (plötzlich) etwas anderes geschah, benutzt du das *past progressive* und das *simple past*.

past progressive	simple past
While Tia **was buying** a drink	the live music **started**.
Were the children **eating** their food	**when** Sam Albright **arrived**?

was gerade passierte: *past progressive* → neues Ereignis: *simple past*

8 MENGENANGABEN

quantifiers TB p. 151

Mengenangaben verwendest du, wenn du keine genaue Menge oder Anzahl von etwas nennen möchtest.

Much, *many* und *a lot of* sind Mengenangaben, die man vor allem in Fragen und verneinten Aussagesätzen verwendet.
Much (auf Deutsch „viel“) wird mit Nomen verwendet, die nicht zählbar sind: We haven't got much time.
Many (auf Deutsch „viele“) wird mit Nomen verwendet, die zählbar sind: How many apps have you got on your phone?

In bejahten Aussagesätzen verwendet man eher *a lot of* oder lots of. Hier braucht man nicht zwischen zählbaren und nicht zählbaren Nomen zu unterscheiden: He has lots of advice for a lot of problems.

Auch die Indefinitpronomen *some* und *any* sind Mengenangaben. Auf Deutsch bedeuten *some* und *any* so viel wie „einige“, „ein paar“ oder „etwas“.
In bejahten Aussagesätzen verwendest du *some*: I shared some pictures online.
In verneinten Aussagesätzen und bei den meisten Fragen verwendest du *any*:
Did you take any photos? No, I didn't take any photos.

9 DIE STEIGERUNG VON ADJEKTIVEN

the comparison of adjectives TB p. 152

Möchtest du Personen oder Dinge vergleichen, kannst du Adjektive steigern.

Einsilbige und einige zweisilbige Adjektive werden durch das Anhängen von *-er* und *-est* gesteigert:
Belfast is big,
Glasgow is bigger,
but London is biggest.

Mehrsilbige Adjektive werden mit *more* und *most* gesteigert:
Our trip was boring,
my friend's trip was more boring,
but my parent's trip was most boring.

Bei manchen Adjektiven ändert sich die Schreibweise (z. B. *big – bigger*, *easy – easier*, *nice – nicer*) und einige haben unregelmäßige Formen, die du lernen musst wie Vokabeln, z. B.: *good – better – (the) best* *bad – worse – (the) worst*.

In Vergleichssätzen benutzt du den Komparativ mit *than*: It was bigger than I expected.
Sind die Eigenschaften gleich, benutzt du *as … as*: The cows are as funny and cool as in the pictures.

10 POSSESSIVPRONOMEN

possessive pronouns TB p. 153

Du kennst bereits die Possessivbegleiter (*my*, *your*, …). Sie zeigen an, wem etwas gehört. Possessivpronomen (*mine*, *yours*, …) benutzt du, wenn du ein Nomen mit Possessivbegleiter, das bereits genannt wurde, nicht wiederholen möchtest.

My sandcastle has got more towers. → Mine has got more towers.

Yours is bigger, Declan. I think Tia should win: hers has got more details. Ours are pretty good, too!

11 DAS PERFEKT: AUSSAGEN

the present perfect: statements TB p. 154

Das *present perfect* verwendest du, wenn etwas irgendwann in einem Zeitraum von der Vergangenheit bis zur Gegenwart passiert ist sowie wenn ein Vorgang in der Vergangenheit noch Auswirkungen auf die Gegenwart hat. Du bildest es mit *have / has* + Partizip Perfekt (*past participle*) oder den entsprechenden Kurzformen. Bei regelmäßigen Verben bildest du das Partizip Perfekt, indem du an die Grundform des Verbs die Endung *-ed* anhängst: Die Formen der unregelmäßigen Verben musst du auswendig lernen wie Vokabeln.

You have just arrived.
She has prepared some lunch.

They have been on a city tour.
She has already told him about it.

Die Verneinung bildest du mit *haven't / hasn't* + Partizip Perfekt:

I haven't been to a wedding.
He hasn't visited London.

They've never eaten haggis.
I have never met a famous person.

12 DAS PERFEKT: FRAGEN

the present perfect: questions TB p. 155

Mit einer Entscheidungsfrage im *present perfect* kannst du z. B. nachfragen, ob jemand etwas in der Vergangenheit schon einmal gemacht hat. Du bildest sie, indem du *have* oder *has* an den Satzanfang stellst.

Have you heard of haggis, neeps and tatties?	Yes, I have.	No, I haven't.
Has your sister ever met a famous person?	Yes, she has.	No, she hasn't.

Bei Fragen mit Fragewort steht das Fragewort am Satzanfang: **Where** have you been? **What** have you already bought?

Bei Fragen und Aussagen werden häufig Adverbien der unbestimmten Zeit verwendet, z. B. *ever* (= jemals), *never* (= nie), *already* (= schon), *just* (= gerade) und *not yet* (= noch nicht). Die meisten Adverbien stehen direkt vor dem Partizip Perfekt:
Have you ever been to London? – No, I've never been there.
Has Dad already done the shopping for Burns Night? – Yes, he has just come back.
Beachte die Ausnahme: *yet* steht am Satzende: Have you ever been to Paris? – No, I haven't been there yet.

Dustys Hinweis

Beachte, dass *'s* beim Perfekt die Kurzform von *has* ist und nicht von *is*!

She's already told him about it. → She has already told him about it.

She's telling him about it right now. → She is telling him about it right now. (*present progressive*).

13 VERBMUSTER
verb patterns TB p. 156

Im Englischen kann nach Verben ein Gerundium oder ein Infinitiv stehen. Bei einigen Verben ist beides möglich, bei anderen nur eine der Formen. Manchmal ändert sich die Bedeutung, je nachdem welche Form man wählt.

Verb + Gerundium: Imagine seeing Nessie tomorrow!

Verb + Infinitiv: They decided to visit the Highlands.

Verb + Gerundium oder Infinitiv ohne Bedeutungsunterschied: She **loves** travelling / to travel.

Verb + Gerundium oder Infinitiv mit Bedeutungsunterschied:

They **forgot** buying a postcard. → Sie haben vergessen, dass sie (schon) eine Postkarte gekauft haben.

They **forgot** to buy a postcard. → Sie haben vergessen, eine Postkarte zu kaufen.

14 DAS FUTUR MIT *WILL*: AUSSAGEN
the will-future: statements TB p. 157

Wenn du über die Zukunft sprechen möchtest, kannst du das *will-future* verwenden. Damit kannst du spontane Entscheidungen ausdrücken oder Vorhersagen machen. Es wird mit *will* und der Grundform des Verbs gebildet. Die Form *will* ist bei allen Personen gleich. Beim Sprechen verwendet man meist die Kurzform *'ll*, beim Schreiben meist die Langform.
Für die Verneinung fügst du *not* hinter *will* ein = *will not*. Die Kurzform ist *won't*.

I will be famous. → I'll be famous.
You will not find it there. → You won't find it there.

We will live in London. → We'll live in London.
There will not be any rain. → There won't be any rain.

15 DAS FUTUR MIT *WILL*: FRAGEN
the will-future: questions TB p. 158

Bei Entscheidungsfragen im *will-future* steht *will* am Satzanfang. Du verwendest *will* bzw. *won't* auch in den Kurzantworten.

Will the weather be good? Yes, it will. | No, it won't.
Will they arrive on time? Yes, they will. | No, they won't.

Bei Fragen mit Fragewort steht das Fragewort am Satzanfang: **Where** will we live in five years? **How long** will it last?

16 DAS FUTUR MIT *GOING TO*: AUSSAGEN
the going to-future: statements TB p. 159

Wenn du über Pläne für die Zukunft sprechen willst, kannst du das *going to*-future verwenden. Man verwendet es auch bei Ereignissen, die wahrscheinlich eintreten werden. Im Deutschen gibt es keine entsprechende Zeitform.
Du bildest das Futur mit *going to* mit einer Form von *be* + *going to* + Grundform des Verbs.
Für die Verneinung stellst du *not* hinter die Form von *be*. Auch hier wird häufig die Kurzform verwendet.

I **am** going to meet them. → I**'m** going to meet them.
You **are** not going to go there. → You**'re** not going to go there.

The club **is** going to visit LA. → The club**'s** going to visit LA.
He **is** not going to come. → He**'s** not going to come.

17 DAS FUTUR MIT *GOING TO*: FRAGEN
the going to-future: questions TB p. 160

Mit einer Frage im *going to-future* kannst du z. B. danach fragen, welche Pläne jemand hat.
Bei Entscheidungsfragen rückt im *going to-future* die Form von *be* (*am*, *is*, *are*) an den Satzanfang. In der Kurzantwort steht dann die entsprechende Form von *be*.

Is her team going to win today? Yes, it is. | No, it isn't.
Are you going to watch the game? Yes, I am. | No, I'm not.

Bei Fragen mit Fragewort steht das Fragewort am Satzanfang: **What** are they going to do? **How** is she going to celebrate?

Dustys Hinweis

Welche Futurform passender ist, hängt meistens vom Kontext ab. Das *going to-future* verwendest du, wenn du über Pläne sprichst. Das *will-future* drückt vor allem aus, dass es sich um eine spontane Entscheidung oder um eine Vorhersage handelt.

I'm going to buy the tickets online. (*Das habe ich so geplant*)

I'll buy the tickets online.
(Ich habe vielleicht gerade gehört, dass die Tickets schnell ausverkauft sind und mich nun spontan entschieden, sie im Voraus zu kaufen.)

Welcome to Edinburgh

1a

Read the text on page 78 in your textbook again. Are the statements right or wrong? Tick (✓).

	right	wrong
1 Holyrood Park is in the Highlands.	☐	☐
2 The UK has always been one country.	☐	☐
3 On the Royal Mile you can go shopping.	☐	☐
4 Some streets in Edinburgh still look like they did 300 years ago.	☐	☐
5 Edinburgh Castle is on Arthur's seat.	☐	☐
6 You can hear the "one o'clock gun" at Edinburgh Castle.	☐	☐
7 Haggis is raw sheep meat with fried carrots.	☐	☐

1b

Read the text again and match the sentence parts. There is one more ending than you need.

1 Arthur's seat is
2 The royal family has
3 The Real Mary King's Close is
4 You can find the UK's oldest crown jewels at
5 The "one o'clock gun" helped people

A a palace in Scotland.
B to tell the time.
C the Scottish word for little lakes.
D an old volcano.
E Edinburgh Castle.
F an underground version of the Royal Mile.

1c

Write your own sentence for the ending you didn't need in 1b.

____

What do you need for Scottish porridge?

2

Read the recipe on page 79 in your textbook again. Find suitable words for these ingredients.

1 ____________________

2 ____________________

3 ____________________

 / 

4 ____________ or ____________

 / 

5 ____________ or ____________

A song

3 audio 2/8, grammar in short: 12 present perfect

Read and listen to the song on page 80 in your textbook again. Find suitable questions for these pictures.

0

1

2

3

4

5

0 *Have you ever been to Paris?*

1 ______

2 ______

3 ______

4 ______

5 ______

Lots of questions

4a grammar in short: 12 present perfect

Complete the questions. Choose a verb from the box and put it in the *present perfect*.

cook · be · forget · eat · meet · visit

1 Have you ever ______ to Berlin?

2 Have you ever ______ a famous person?

3 Have you ever ______ Edinburgh Castle?

4 Have you ever ______ dinner for your family?

5 Have you ever ______ porridge?

6 Have you ever ______ your homework?

4b grammar in short: 11 present perfect

Write down your short answers to the questions in 4a. Then ask a partner and write down his or her short answers.

	my answers	my partner's answers
1	______	______
2	______	______
3	______	______
4	______	______
5	______	______
6	______	______

Tasty food

5a

Read the sentences and write down the correct food. The pictures will help you.

1 You can have these mashed, for example. → ______

2 You can put this in tea or on your cereal. → ______

3 You can fry or scramble these and have them for breakfast. → ______

4 You eat these with haggis and potatoes. → ______

5 You can put this on toast for a sweet breakfast. → ______

6 You can have this deep-fried in Scotland. → ______

5b

Write your own sentences like in 5a for different types of food. Then read them out to a partner. Can he or she guess which food you are describing?

1 ______

2 ______

3 ______

A second trip to Loch Ness

1a skill: writing TB p.165

Look at the pictures to find out about Tia and Jack's second trip to Loch Ness. Tick (✓) the correct sentence for each picture.

1

- ☐ Tia and Jack went home.
- ☐ Tia and Jack went back to Loch Ness.
- ☐ Tia and Jack visited the shop at Loch Ness.

2

- ☐ They had lunch at the lake.
- ☐ They went swimming in the lake.
- ☐ They looked for the monster in the lake.

3

- ☐ They ran away.
- ☐ They saw something strange in the lake.
- ☐ Jack dropped his phone in the lake.

1b

Write a story based on the pictures in 1a. Give your story a title and write an ending. Write about 100 words.

Title: ______________________

____

____

____

____

____

____

1c

Read your partner's text. Fill in the checklist.

		yes	no
1	Your story has got a nice title.	☐	☐
2	You have included every picture in your story.	☐	☐
3	You have used two or more linking words (e.g. next, before, however, then, ...)	☐	☐
4	You have used some adjectives (e.g. big, small, old, new, nice, ...)	☐	☐
5	You have used a question (?) and/or an exclamation (!).	☐	☐
6	The tenses are correct.	☐	☐

Personal comment: I think your story is ______________________!

Did you know?

2a audio 2/10

Listen to the first part of the podcast. Which words are mentioned? Tick (✓).

☐ lakes ☐ monster ☐ kilometres ☐ exciting ☐ wonderful

2b audio 2/11

Listen to the second part of the podcast. Answer the questions.

1 What is Cherry Island?

2 Why can't you see very far into the water?

3 Why do Elaine and Rory want to go to Urquhart Castle later in the afternoon?

A boat tour

3

Lies den Flyer über eine Bootstour, den du in einem Hotel am Loch Ness gefunden hast. Bearbeite die Aufgaben stichpunktartig auf Deutsch. Ein Wort genügt nicht.

Exciting Boat Tour on Loch Ness

Have you ever wanted to go on a boat tour on a beautiful lake? Then join us on our special boat tour on Loch Ness in Scotland! You can join our boat tour every hour between 10 a.m. and 6 p.m. In summer, we have an evening tour at 8 p.m.
If you love feeling the cool wind on your face, you can sit at the front of the boat. If you don't enjoy being cold, you can also sit inside the boat. We also serve cold drinks and snacks on board the boat in case you start to get hungry! You can buy tickets on the day of the tour. If you want to avoid waiting in long queues (especially in summer), you can buy a ticket online now. You can find the QR code to our website on the other side of this flyer.
Most importantly: Remember to bring your camera – just in case Nessie decides to say hello ...

1 Zu welchen Uhrzeiten finden die Touren statt?

2 Wer sollte besser im Boot sitzen und nicht vorne?

3 Wie kann man Tickets kaufen? (2 Möglichkeiten)

4 Wo findet man den QR Code für die Webseite?

5 Warum sollte man seine Kamera nicht vergessen?

Hello from Scotland

4 grammar in short: 11+12 present perfect

Tia and Jack have sent a postcard to Emma. Fill in the gaps. Choose a suitable verb from the box and put it in the *present perfect*. There are two more verbs than you need.

be · be · buy · come · ~~have~~ · see · swim · try · walk

14th April

Dear Emma,

Hello from Scotland! We have ____had____ *a great time so far. We have just* ________ *back from Loch Ness, but we didn't see Nessie. We have* ________ *lots of different types of food. Haggis is very interesting! We have also* ________ *to Edinburgh Castle and we have* ________ *around Edinburgh. It is a very beautiful city. Have you* ________ *to Edinburgh before? We have also* ________ *you a small present. We will give it to you when we are back.*

See you soon, Tia and Jack x

Emma Blum
147 Camden Road
London
NW1 9HA
United Kingdom

Tourists at Loch Ness

5

Read the sentences and circle the right word.

1 Loch Ness is famous for its monster, Nessie. **Then / However**, nobody knows if Nessie really exists.

2 **After / So** the first photo of Nessie in 1934, many people started to travel to Loch Ness.

3 Loch Ness wasn't a very popular place for tourists **before / next** the photo was published in a newspaper.

4 Many people want to see Nessie, **but / so** they go on boat tours on the lake.

5 **Before / After** you go on a boat tour, you need to first buy a ticket.

6 Lots of tourists hope to see Nessie, **but / before** they usually go home disappointed.

A travel blog

Dusty explains
Pay attention to the linking words. They can help you find the right order.

1a

Look at the parts of the travel blog. Find the right order (1–7).

We were really full so we paid and went for a walk. It wasn't raining anymore. We watched some musicians on the street. ☐

After Edinburgh Castle, we walked into the city and found the Royal Mile. It is a very pretty street with lots of nice shops. Then it started to rain. ☐

Then we got really tired so we have come back to the hotel. I am going to bed now. I can't wait for tomorrow! ☐

Because it was raining, we went into a little restaurant. My dad wanted to try haggis so he ordered that for his dinner. I'm a vegetarian, but they even had vegetarian haggis! It was really tasty. My sister doesn't like trying new food so she had a pizza. ☐

We took the train and we arrived at 2 o'clock in the afternoon. First, we wanted to find our hotel so we could leave our bags and suitcases there. ☐

After the hotel, we walked up to Edinburgh Castle. What a fantastic place! Have you heard about the "one o'clock" gun? You can hear it every day at 1 p.m. We missed it because it was already 3 p.m.! ☐

Hi everyone! Today I would like to tell you all about my first day in Edinburgh. I am here with my dad and my sister. ☐

1b

Imagine you go to Scotland and you want to write a travel blog. Answer these questions to plan your text.

1 Where did you go and who did you go with? ______

2 Which sights did you see? ______

3 What was the weather like? ______

4 What did you eat and drink? ______

5 What was your favourite part? ______

1c

skill: writing TB p. 165

Write a travel blog post based on the information in 1b. Write about 60 words.

Check out

Speaking solutions p. 79

Talk to a partner about what you have already done and what you haven't done yet. You can use the ideas in the box. Take turns.

meet a famous person · walk around Loch Ness · go to a concert · play the bagpipes · go to a wedding · be in hospital · talk to a Scot · take part in a ceilidh · do paddleboarding · be to Edinburgh · try fish and chips

You can say:

I haven't been to Edinburgh yet.
I've already been in hospital.
...
What about you?

I can: say what I have or haven't done before. ◯

Listening audio 2/15, solutions p. 79

Listen and tick (✓) the right answers.

1 Where are they going?
- ☐ Wales
- ☐ Scotland
- ☐ England

2 Where do they go first?
- ☐ Edinburgh
- ☐ Aberdeen
- ☐ Inverness

3 How long does the journey to Inverness take?
- ☐ about five hours
- ☐ about four hours
- ☐ about three hours

4 Where do they need to change trains?
- ☐ Perth
- ☐ Glasgow
- ☐ Aberdeen

5 When do they arrive?
- ☐ around 2 p.m.
- ☐ around 11 a.m.
- ☐ around 1 p.m.

6 What do they want to do when they arrive?
- ☐ meet friends
- ☐ have lunch
- ☐ look for Nessie

I can: understand a dialogue about a trip. ◯

Mediation solutions p. 79

Lies den Infotext. Beantworte die Fragen stichpunktartig auf Deutsch. Ein Wort genügt nicht.

The Real Mary King's Close is a very narrow street in Edinburgh. In the 17th century, it was a normal street, but when another building was built over it in 1760, the close was suddenly underground. Streets were often named after important people who lived there. Mary King was a successful businesswoman in the 1630s, so the close has her name.

1 Was ist das Besondere an der Straße?

____

2 Wie erhielten Straßen früher häufig ihre Namen?

____

3 Warum heißt die Straße "Mary King's Close"?

____

I can: understand relevant information in a text. ◯

Reading solutions p. 79

Read the postcard. Then read the sentences and tick (✓) them right, wrong or not in the text.

Hi Susan!
Greetings from Scotland! We've been lucky: it's been very sunny until now. We are in Edinburgh at the moment. At the weekend we want to go to Loch Ness and look for Nessie. In Edinburgh we've already visited The Real Mary King's Close, the underground street I told you about, and Edinburgh Castle, of course. We've also listened to some bagpipe players and watched some sword dancing. Tomorrow we are going to a Ceilidh! I'm very excited! I love Scottish music and dancing!
Best wishes, Charlie

	✓	✗	---
1 The weather has been bad.			
2 They are looking for Nessie at the moment.			
3 They have already visited Edinburgh Castle.			
4 They have not visited The Real Mary King's Close yet.			
5 They have not tried haggis yet.			
6 Charlie loves Scottish music and dancing.			

I can: understand a postcard from Scotland. ◯

Writing solutions p. 79

You have recently been on holiday in Scotland. Write an email to your English friend. Tell him or her about:

- what you did
- a little problem
- the food you tried

Don't forget to give some extra information and a personal comment. Write 60 words or more.

____

____

____

____

____

____

I can: write an email about holidays in Scotland. ◯

USE OF ENGLISH

Grammar solutions p. 79

Form sentences in the *present perfect*.

0 Jack – never – visit – Edinburgh Castle *Jack has never visited Edinburgh Castle.*

1 Gemma – already – play – the bagpipes ______________________________

2 Charlie – recently – be – to a ceilidh ______________________________

3 Sue and Gordon – cook – haggis – for their family ______________________________

4 Mara – already – finish – her homework ______________________________

Vocabulary solutions p. 79

Fill in the gaps with the right words.

1 An event where two people get married is called a ______________________ .

2 Loch Ness and the Chiemsee are ______________________ .

3 The Scottish word for "potato" is ______________________ .

4 Together, the years from 1900 to 1990 are called the 20th ______________________ .

5 When you want to stay in a hotel or guesthouse, you need to ______________________ a room.

6 ______________________ is the Scottish word for "boy".

I can: write about what somebody has / hasn't done. ◯ understand new words. ◯

Preparing for the United States

1

Read the text on page 94 in your textbook again. Tick (✓) the correct ending of the sentence. Sometimes more than one answer is correct.

1 Every state in the USA ...

☐ ... has its own laws. ☐ ... has its own government. ☐ ... has its own capital.

2 Most people live ...

☐ ... in the north and south. ☐ ... in the east and west. ☐ ... in the east and south.

3 Miami is famous for ...

☐ ... its beaches. ☐ ... the good weather. ☐ ... creative people.

4 In the Midwest there is ...

☐ ... lots of space. ☐ ... a big river. ☐ ... a beautiful beach.

5 In the USA you can find the place with the most ...

☐ ... sun on earth. ☐ ... snow on earth. ☐ ... tornadoes on earth.

Stamford climate

2

Jack informiert sich über das Klima in Stamford. Lies den Text und kreuze an, ob die Aussagen richtig, falsch oder nicht im Text zu finden sind.

Stamford, Connecticut, USA

Stamford is in the northeast. Its climate is classified as warm and temperate. There is significant rainfall throughout the year in Stamford. Even the driest month still has a lot of rainfall. The average annual temperature in Stamford is 52.4°F. In a year, the total rainfall is around 45.2 inches.

	right	wrong	not in the text
1 Das Klima in Stamford wird als kalt und trocken beschrieben.	☐	☐	☐
2 Die Landwirtschaft in Stamford leidet unter dem Klima.	☐	☐	☐
3 Es regnet das ganze Jahr über viel in Stamford.	☐	☐	☐
4 Nur im trockensten Monat gibt es keinen Niederschlag.	☐	☐	☐
5 Die Durchschnittstemperatur beträgt 45,2°.	☐	☐	☐
6 Der durchschnittliche Niederschlag liegt über 45 Zoll.	☐	☐	☐
7 Es fließt ein Fluss durch Stamford.	☐	☐	☐

Jack's host family replies

3 grammar in short: 14 will-future

The Wright family wrote Jack back. What did they say? Complete the sentences with the correct form of the verbs in the box. Use the *will-future*.

show you around · be a wonderful experience · help with the household tasks · see you at the airport · be a great way to make new friends

New Message

To: wrights@stamford.com

Subject: RE: Hello from the Wright Family

Dear Jack,

We received your email and we are very excited about your visit. We think that learning about each other's cultures ______________________. We are sure you will adapt to our family's routines. We believe that working together as a team is important, so we are glad you ______________________. There are many different activities and clubs available at the high school. Sarah and Jayden go there, too and they ______________________. You can learn more about American culture outside of the classroom and this ______________________. Your arrival is just a few days away and we ______________________!

Sincerely yours, The Wright Family

Will or won't?

4 grammar in short: 14 will-future

Fill in the gaps with the right form of the verbs from the box. There are more words than you need.

not get · make · not know · feel · live · be · not forget · help

1 In most exchanges a student ______________ with a host family in their house.

2 Usually the host family ______________ a special meal to welcome the exchange student.

3 In the beginning, an exchange student ______________ some of the rules at home.

4 If the host family and the student speak different languages, it ______________ hard to talk at first.

5 There is so much to see and do during the exchange – it ______________ boring!

6 The host family and the exchange student ______________ the experience.

A weather song

5 audio 2/21

Listen to the weather song and sing along. Then write another verse to the song. Make sure the last word for each pair of sentences rhymes.

Wake up in the morning, what do you see?
Clouds, rain or sun, what will it be?
Will it be a windy, grey or sunny day?
Grab an umbrella or shades, either way!

Weather, weather, dancing on the ground,
Mother nature's all around.
Weather, weather, what's in store today?
Wear the right clothes and go and play!

When it's hot, you feel the heat,
And all your ice cream melts on your feet.
When it's chilly, wear a sweater.
In no time you'll feel so much better.

Weather, weather, dancing on the ground,
Mother nature's all around.
Weather, weather, what's in store today?
Wear the right clothes and go and play!

Weather, weather, changing every day,
Foggy, misty, clear or grey.
Weather, weather, what will you say?
Ready for tomorrow, come rain or sunny day!

Weather on another planet

6 skill: writing TB p. 165

You are an astronaut and you visit the planet of Lumara for the first time. The planet's weather is completely different from Earth's. Write a short text about it for the people back home. Write about 60 words. Write about:

- what the planet of Lumara looks like from space.
- what the temperature is like.
- what colour the sky is during the day and at night.
- a special weather event on Lumara that does not happen on Earth.
- how you like the planet of Lumara.

Jack's email

1a

Read Jack's email on page 98 in your textbook again. Which heading fits best for which paragraph (1–5)? Be careful, there are more headings than paragraphs.

☐ Introducing Stamford
☐ A great trip
☐ How to protect the environment
☐ A special training
☐ Going to the movies
☐ Jack's host family

1b wordbank: living in the USA TB p. 182 and acting green TB p. 185

Find the odd word out and explain it.

1 urban farm – green roof – host family – rainwater
2 compost – BBQ – breakfast – lunch
3 duplex – backyard – house – tornado
4 tornado drill – shopping mall – safe zone – alarm

1 ______
2 ______
3 ______
4 ______

Writing an email

2a

Read Jack's email on page 98 in your textbook again. Write down the lines of the different parts.

1 greeting ______
2 introduction ______
3 main body ______
4 closing ______
5 saying good-bye ______
6 writer's name ______

2b

Look at the email on page 98 in your textbook again. Find and write down:

1 a sentence in the future: ______
2 a question in the future: ______
3 linking words: ______

2c skill: writing TB p. 165

Now imagine you are Tia. Answer Jack's email. Tell him what you find interesting about his stay in the USA and answer his questions. You can use the phrases from the box.

New Message

To: jack@camdenroad.com

Subject: Hi brother

____

____

____

____

____

____

____

You can write:

Hi, / Hi … / Dear …,
How are you? / How are things? / How's it going?
It was good /nice /great to hear from you.
I was so surprised to hear that …
Say hello to …
I'll try and phone you at the weekend.
Hope to hear from you soon. / See you soon. /
Write back soon.
Love, / Lots of love, / All the best, / Take care, /
Best wishes,

British or American?

3a audio 2/23

Listen to Jack and Sarah and tick (✓) whether the words have a British or an American pronunciation.

	British	American		British	American
1 fɑːrm	☐	☐	5 həʊst	☐	☐
2 ˈsɪstə	☐	☐	6 tɔrˈneɪdoʊs	☐	☐
3 ɪkˈsaɪtɪŋ	☐	☐	7 ˈtuzdeɪ	☐	☐
4 ˈreɪnwɑːdər	☐	☐	8 tjuːb	☐	☐

3b

Compare your answers to 3a with a partner. Which four differences do you notice about British and American pronunciation? Talk about it and write down your results.

1 ______________________________

2 ______________________________

3 ______________________________

4 ______________________________

What will happen to the polar bears?

4 grammar in short: 15 will-future

Fill in the gaps with the right form of the verbs in brackets. Use the *will-future*.

Harlan: Hi Jayla, ______________________________ (you, be) at the Green Club tomorrow?

Jayla: No, I won't be there. Oh, you're giving your talk about Arctic polar bears, right? Maybe you can tell me a little bit about it now. ______________________________ (how, you, start)?

Harlan: First, I'll show a video of a hungry polar bear. Then I'll ask a question: ______________________________ (what, happen) to the polar bears if we don't do anything in the coming years?

Jayla: ______________________________ (they, disappear)?

Harlan: Yes, they'll disappear by 2100 if we don't do anything.

Jayla: That's terrible. ______________________________ (what, you, say) next?

Harlan: I'll say that experts believe that the ice in the southern Arctic will soon disappear completely.

Jayla: ______________________________ (what effect, it, have) on the polar bears?

Harlan: They can't find food. But a group of scientists want to move the bears to icy areas further north.

Jayla: Wow! ______________________________ (how, they, do) that?

Harlan: Well, they'll need a lot of support and money, so I am trying to help with that.

Jayla: ______________________________ (you, present) a way to help?

Harlan: Of course I will.

Storm hunters

5

Beschreibe stichpunktartig auf Deutsch, wer *storm hunters* sind und was sie machen. Ein Wort genügt nicht.

A **storm hunter**, often called a storm chaser, drives into the path of extreme weather events to study, document, and understand these phenomena. Tornadoes are often the primary targets for many storm hunters. They can see tornadoes of different sizes, from thin rope tornadoes to enormous ones shaped like an ice cream cone.

____

____

____

____

____

In New York City

1a

Read the text on page 102 in your textbook again. Cross out the wrong information and correct it.

0 The *Green Club* went to New York City to study ~~art~~. urban sustainability

1 There is not much need for water and heating in a passive house. ______

2 NYC does a lot to protect motorbike riders. ______

3 There is a green roof and an urban farm on Javits Center. ______

4 The zoo of the park supports birds, insects, and other wildlife. ______

5 The students learned about animals at the urban farm. ______

1b

Draw the *Green Club's* route through NYC from Times Square to the The High Line on the map. Then use an online map to answer the questions.

1 How long does the train from Stamford to NYC take?

______

2 Which subway goes from 425 Grand Concourse to Times Square?

______

3 How long does it take to walk from the Empire State Building to the High Line?

______

4 The group visited Liberty Island. Which other islands are there in the bay?

______

Tour of a green roof

2 audio 2/25

Listen to the tour guide talk about the green roof at the Javits Center and answer Jack and Sarah's questions.

1 Has the number of birds and insects changed since you built the roof?

______

2 Are the solar panels on the roof enough to power the whole Javits Center?

______

3 How much money does the Center save by saving energy?

______

4 Can a school create a green roof?

______

The Statue of Liberty

3

Lies den *social media post* der *Statue of Liberty – Ellis Island Foundation*. Finde und korrigiere die Fehler in den deutschen Sätzen.

← → ↻ – ×

As there have been a lot of enquiries about our tickets recently, here is a compilation of answers to the most frequently asked questions:
- There are three different types of tickets: general admission, pedestal reserve, crown reserve
- With the general admission you can only visit the Statue of Liberty Museum and Grounds and the Ellis Island National Museum of Immigration
- The round trip ferry service is included in all of the tickets
- When choosing your reservation date and time, this is your entry into the Security Facility – not the ferry departure and not the entry time to the statue! The waiting time can be several hours.

#FAQ #statueellisfdn #statueellisnps 🗽 ❤️

0 Im *post* geht es um ~~Probleme beim Ticketkauf~~.

häufig gestellte Fragen zu den Tickets

1 Es gibt fünf verschiedene Arten von Tickets.

______

2 Mit dem allgemeinen Ticket kann man die Krone der Freiheitsstatue besuchen.

______

3 Die Fähre muss extra gebucht werden.

______

4 Die Zeit, die auf dem Ticket steht, zeigt an, wann man die Freiheitsstatue betritt.

______

My visit to the Statue of Liberty

4 skill: writing TB p. 165

Write a diary entry about a visit to the Statue of Liberty. Describe:

- **how you got there.**
- **a funny situation.**
- **what you liked best.**

Don't forget to give some extra information and a personal comment. Write 60 words or more.

You can write:

Dear diary,
Guess where I was today …
We saw / experienced / did / went on / …
I think …

A sustainable city

5

Look at exercise 4 on page 104 in your textbook again. Fill in the gaps with the right words.

In Stamford, Connecticut, people care about the ______________ .

Many of them use ______________ to get energy from the sun. This type of energy is called ______________ because the sun rises again every day. Stamford has also got an urban farm where the community can grow their own food and learn about healthy eating. The farm is a good example of ______________ because it recycles food waste, offers local food without a big transportation system and helps the ______________ like bees, birds and butterflies.

So, although Stamford is an ______________ area with many buildings and people, the city tries to be as eco-friendly as possible.

Our future

6 grammar in short: 14+15 will-future

What do you think the future will be like? What will you be and do? Draw a picture and write about it.

You can write about:

- means of transport
- food and drink
- houses and other buildings
- electronic devices
- clothes
- ...

More practice: guided writing

1a skill: writing TB p. 165

Imagine you went to NYC with Jack and the *Green Club* last week. Write an email about the trip to your English pen friend and tell them:

- **which sights you visited**
- **what you learned about sustainability**
- **how you liked the trip**

Write 60 words or more.

New Message

To: myfriend@camdenroad.com

Subject: My trip to NYC

1b

Swap your text with a partner. Read your partner's text and fill in the checklist.

	yes	no
1 You have included all three aspects in your email.	☐	☐
2 You have followed the structure of an email.	☐	☐
3 Your grammar is correct.	☐	☐
4 Your spelling is correct.	☐	☐

Personal comment:

This is really good: ______

You could improve: ______

Check out

Speaking solutions p. 81

Work with a partner. Choose a place and tell your partner what the weather will be like on Saturday.

New York City, NY	Stamford, CT	Yuma, AZ	Los Angeles, CA
59°F	37°F	80°F	76°F

I can: talk about the weather. ◯

Listening audio 2/28, solutions p. 81

Listen to the dialogue and answer the questions.

1 Who has a good idea for making the school more sustainable?

______

2 What is the idea?

______

3 What does Terry think about it?

______

4 What does Amy suggest students get for ten points?

______

5 What do they want to do next?

______

I can: understand a dialogue on sustainability. ◯

Mediation solutions p. 81

Mache dir stichpunktartig Notizen zum Poster auf Deutsch. Ein Wort genügt nicht.

The green and fun way to get from A to B in NYC!
There are three ways to rent one of our 10,000 bikes:
- Monthly subscription: $ 28.20 / month
- Pay as you go: A classic bike is only $ 0.20 / minute. The first 30 minutes of your ride are always free!
- Unlimited passes:
  Day pass: $ 19 / day OR Weekly pass: only $ 99!

We have more than 1000 stations all across the city where you can pick up and drop off your bike.

1 Was kostet $ 28.20 im Monat? ______
2 Anzahl Fahrräder: ______
3 Erste halbe Stunde kostet: ______
4 Ein Wochenticket kostet: ______
5 Anzahl Leihstationen: ______

I can: understand a poster in English. ◯

Reading solutions p. 81

Read the email and answer the questions. Underline the answers in the text and write down the number.

New Message
To: myfriend@camdenroad.com
Subject: My school day

Hi Jen,
Thank you very much for your email!
You asked what I usually[0] do after school. Well, mostly I go to an after-school club. On Mondays, there's Cooking Club. On Tuesdays, I go to the Theater Club. And on Fridays, I've got Green Club. Do you have clubs at your school? And if yes, do you have a favorite?
My favorite is the Theater Club. I also often meet my friends after school or after the clubs. We go to the movies or just hang out at the mall. What do you do after school? Looking forward to your next message!
Best wishes, Oliver

0 What is Oliver writing about?
1 What does he usually do after school?
2 What does he do on Tuesdays?
3 What does he also often do?
4 Where does he go with his friends?
5 What questions does he ask Jen?

I can: understand an email about life in the USA. ◯

Writing solutions p. 81

You want to start a Green Club at your school. Write a blog entry about green projects you could do. Write about:

- how another Green Club has given you ideas
- an activity you want to do
- when you want to start

Don't forget to give some extra information and a personal comment. Write 60 words or more.

____

____

____

____

____

I can: write about sustainability. ◯

USE OF ENGLISH

Grammar solutions p. 81

a) Fill in the right future form. Use *will-future, present progressive* or *simple present with future meaning*.

1 The school bus ____________ (leave) at 7 a.m.
2 I think you ____________ (like) the food there.
3 We (visit) ____________ my grandma tomorrow.
4 Oliver and his friends ____________ (go) to the movies after school tomorrow.
5 The concert ____________ (start) at 6 p.m.
6 It ____________ (be) so much fun!
7 The friends ____________ (meet) this afternoon.
8 My mum thinks it ____________ (be) too cold to meet outside.

b) Sort the sentences from a) into the table.

predictions / instant decisions	scheduled events	plans
	The school bus leaves at 7 a.m.	

Vocabulary solutions p. 81

Complete the sentences with the right British and American words.

1 British people call them crisps, and Americans call them ____________ .
2 Americans go to the movies: Brits go to the ____________ .
3 In American English they are called ____________ . In Britain people call them trainers.
4 In America, people take a vacation. In Britain, they go on ____________ .

I can: write about the future. ◯ compare British and American English. ◯

A typical day at school

1

Read the blog on pages 114–115 in your textbook again. Complete the sentences.

1 Jack wants to tell people about ______________________________ .

2 On the school bus, Jack ______________________________ .

3 When he gets to school, Jack ______________________________ .

4 Jack's schedule is easy to remember because ______________________________ .

5 On Friday, Jack is going to support ______________________________ .

6 Jack's friends are going to make him jealous because ______________________________ .

Join the club

2

Schaue dir das Poster an. Bearbeite die Aufgaben. Sind die Aussagen richtig, falsch oder nicht im Text?

Green Club Green Club

Ready to grow beyond the classroom?

Join the Green Club!

The club looks after the school's garden, greenhouse and green wall.

Last year, we grew 30 lbs of vegetables that students ate in the cafeteria. We also gave presentations to classes about how to be greener in our daily lives.

Find us in the greenhouse or garden after school on Tuesdays and Thursdays. Everyone is welcome!

Take some seeds and start your own flower garden:

	richtig	falsch	nicht im Text
1 Der *Green Club* trifft sich jeden Tag nach der Schule.	☐	☐	☐
2 Der Club hat letztes Jahr 30 Pfund Gemüse angebaut.	☐	☐	☐
3 Clubmitglieder haben letztes Jahr auch Obst angebaut.	☐	☐	☐
4 Der Club kümmert sich um die *green wall* in der Schule.	☐	☐	☐
5 Neue Mitglieder erhalten eine Anleitung für einen eigenen Blumengarten.	☐	☐	☐
6 Der Club stellt Blumensamen zur Verfügung, damit Schüler ihre eigenen Blumen pflanzen können.	☐	☐	☐
7 Der Club nimmt nur ältere Schüler auf.	☐	☐	☐
8 Der Club organisiert Ausflüge zum botanischen Garten.	☐	☐	☐

Morning announcements

3a audio 2/33

Listen to the announcements at Stamford Middle School. Put them in the correct order.

- [0] Pledge of Allegiance
- [ ] swim team
- [ ] holiday bake sale
- [ ] chess tournament
- [ ] Seaside Center trip
- [ ] eco club meeting
- [ ] yearbook meeting

3b audio 2/33

Listen again. Tick (✓) the correct answer.

1 When is the Green Club meeting today?
- [ ] after school
- [ ] at lunch
- [ ] in 10 minutes

2 What should students bring to the bake sale?
- [ ] $20
- [ ] cake
- [ ] $2

3 When is the next yearbook meeting?
- [ ] next week
- [ ] after school
- [ ] tomorrow

4 Which swim team won at the qualifiers yesterday?
- [ ] the boys' team
- [ ] the girls' team
- [ ] both teams

5 Who can compete at the chess tournament?
- [ ] everyone
- [ ] members of the chess team
- [ ] students at Rippowam Middle School

6 Where do grade 7 students need to go at lunch to join a field trip?
- [ ] room 140
- [ ] room 114
- [ ] room 104

Odd one out

4 wordbank: American school life TB p. 184

Circle the odd one out in each line and think of a suitable word instead.

1 American flag | desk | chair | school bus ____________

2 school spirit | cafeteria | classroom | hall ____________

3 history | announcements | geography | math ____________

4 robotics | green club | restroom | chorus ____________

5 period | elective | class | locker ____________

6 math | English | bus ride | science ____________

A school crossword

5 wordbank: American school life TB p. 184

Complete the crossword.

ACROSS →

2 ____ is another word for a lesson.
4 In ____ you study maps and learn about countries and other places.
5 ____ is another word for timetable.
8 Americans spell "favourite" like this: ____ .

DOWN ↓

1 You can do your homework or use the books in the ____ .
3 You need a ____ to go to the restroom during a lesson.
6 ____ is a school club where you can sing with others.
7 In ____ you work with numbers and solve problems.

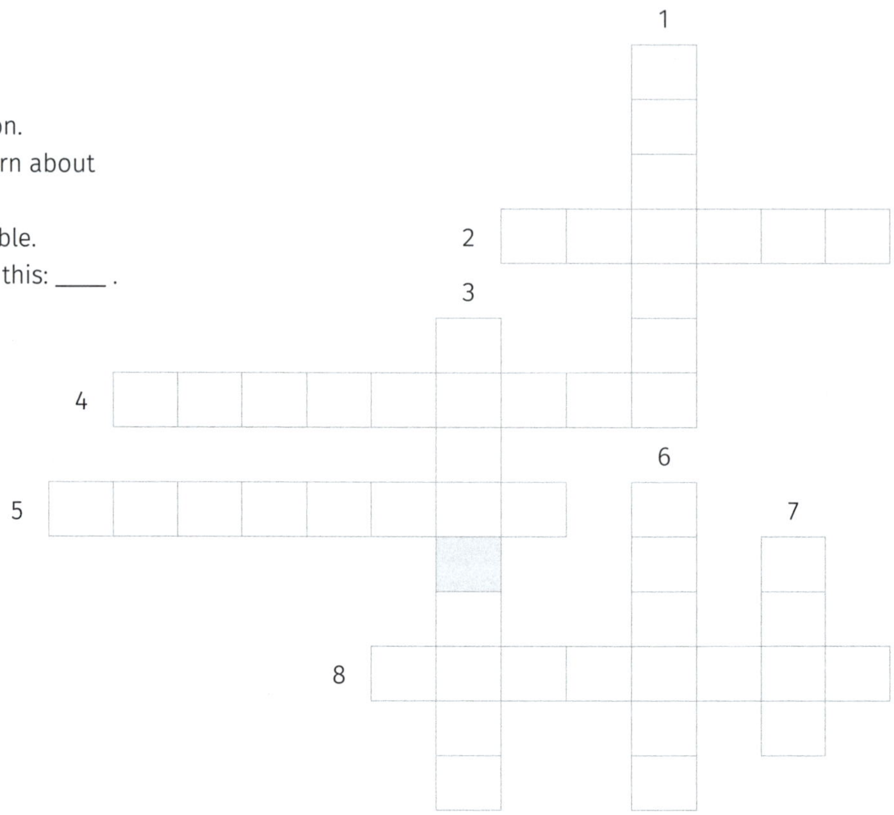

Plans for the Green Club

6 grammar in short: 16 going to-future

Look at the Green Club's plans for the next school year. Rewrite them in complete sentences. Use the *going to-future*.

0 Grow more vegetables *The club is going to grow more vegetables.*

1 Give away seeds for home gardens ____________________

2 Not spend any money on advertising ____________________

3 Look for more guest speakers ____________________

4 Not ignore new students' ideas ____________________

5 Serve more vegetables in the school cafeteria ____________________

____

6 Not organize workshops the day before a holiday ____________________

____

A super event

1

Read the story on page 118 in your textbook again. In which line(s) can you find the following information?

0 Sarah's dad didn't expect to win the radio competition. line 4

1 Sarah doesn't have to wait long to go to the game. ______

2 It is Sarah's first time at a big football game. ______

3 Sarah can see her team really well. ______

4 The half-time show lasts a quarter of an hour. ______

5 It is not clear until the end of the game who is going to win. ______

6 Sarah is worrying that her team might lose. ______

After the game

2 skill: writing TB p. 165

Look at the pictures and tell the story. What happened? Write about 60 words or more.

1

2

3

A phone call with a friend

3a audio 2/35

Listen to Bill's phone call with his friend about the football game. Tick (✓) the things they talk about.

- ☐ the price of the tickets
- ☐ the atmosphere at the game
- ☐ the half-time show
- ☐ snacks at the game
- ☐ the celebration after the game
- ☐ plans to meet

3b audio 2/35

Listen again. Are the sentences right or wrong? Tick (✓).

		right	wrong
1	Bill's friend Ben went to the football game, too.	☐	☐
2	Lots of people were there to support the football teams.	☐	☐
3	The school band played at half-time.	☐	☐
4	There were fireworks in the half-time show.	☐	☐
5	Bill's team lost the game.	☐	☐
6	Bill didn't have fun at the game because his team lost.	☐	☐
7	Ben wants to go to the next game.	☐	☐
8	The friends are going to watch a movie tonight.	☐	☐

Stadium rules

4a

Read the stadium rules. Match the signs (1-6) and the rules.

1 

2 

3 

4 

5 

6 

_____ Always have your ticket ready at the entrance and follow the security rules. This includes a bag check.

_____ You cannot bring outside food and drinks, large bags, or fireworks into the stadium.

_____ The stadium is a smoke-free zone, including e-cigarettes and vapes.

_____ Use trash cans and recycling bins.

_____ In case of an emergency, stay calm, listen to announcements, and follow the directions of stadium staff and security staff.

_____ Never throw objects onto the field, stage, or at other guests.

4b

Lies die Regeln in Aufgabe 4a noch einmal. Bearbeite die Aufgaben stichpunktartig auf Deutsch. Ein Wort genügt nicht.

1 An welcher Stelle werden Taschen zur Sicherheit durchsucht?

____

2 Was darf man nicht ins Stadion mitbringen? Nenne drei Gegenstände.

____

3 Wie kann man seinen Müll im Stadion loswerden?

____

4 Was soll man in Notfallsituationen tun?

____

4c skill: working with words TB p. 162

Now make a word web about stadium rules. Then explain your words to a partner and compare your word webs.

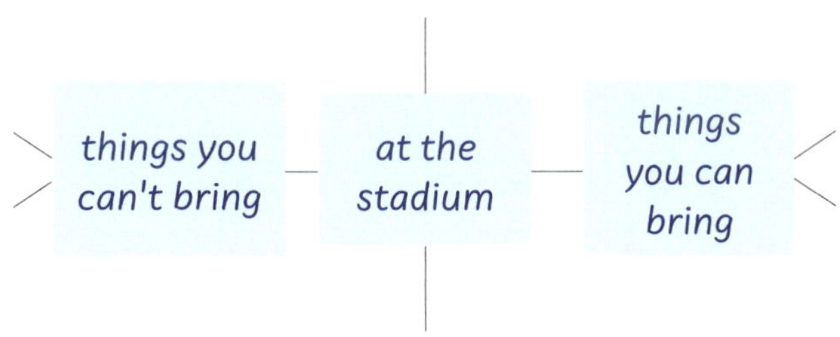

Questions

5 grammar in short: 17 going to-future

Complete the questions with the correct form of the verb in brackets. Use the *going to-future*.

0 *Are you going to go* (**you, go**) to the football game tonight?

1 ______________________ (**who, buy**) tickets for the game?

2 ______________________ (**your girlfriend, come**) with us?

3 What snacks ______________________ (**you, take**)?

4 Why ______________________ (**your parents, not drive**) you to the stadium?

5 ______________________ (**I, need**) money for souvenirs?

A trip to the west coast

1a

Read the text on page 122 in your textbook again. Tick (✓) the sentence which summarises the text best.

- ☐ Along the east coast
- ☐ Walking with giants
- ☐ A nice, long holiday
- ☐ Green travel and green projects

1b

Fill in the gaps with words from Sarah's travel diary on page 122.

1 Using ______________________ bags can help reduce rubbish.

2 You can use the sun's energy to make electricity by putting ______________________ on your roof.

3 ______________________ cars and buses can be a more sustainable way to travel.

4 More and more people want to live in a ______________________ way – using natural products and energy in ways that don't harm the environment.

5 Solar and wind energy are examples of ______________________ energy.

6 We need to protect animals' natural environments, like ______________________ and ______________________ .

7 There are lots of products, like soaps, which are made from ______________________ materials.

Similar word, different meaning

Dusty explains

A *prefix* is a group of letters you add to the start of a word, like *re–* or *un–*. You add a *suffix* to the end of a word.

2a

Look at the rows of words below. The words in each row have the same root. Circle the roots of the words. Then underline the prefixes and suffixes in the words in 1c in green.

0 use useful useless reuse

1 help helpful helpless

2 new renew

3 sustainable unsustainable

2b

Look at the words in 2a again. How do the underlined parts change the meaning of the words? Talk to a partner.

2c

Find two more sets of words with the same root and the prefixes *re–* or *un–*, or suffixes *–ful* or *–less*. You can look in your textbook or in a dictionary. Write them down and explain the meanings to your partner.

1 ____

2 ____

National parks in the USA

3 video 23

Schaue dir das Video an. Vervollständige die Notizen stichpunktartig auf Deutsch. Ein Wort genügt nicht.

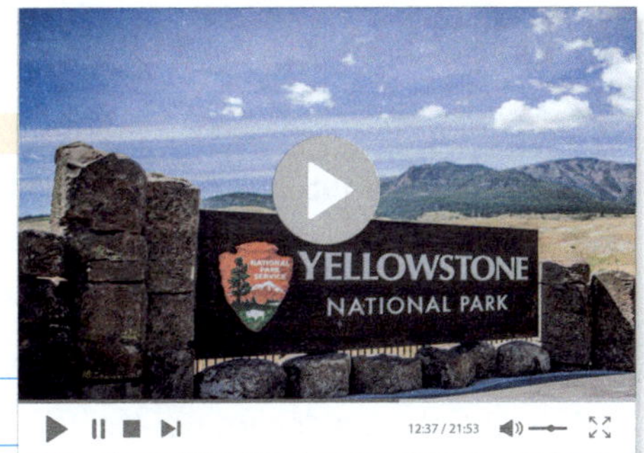

Nationalparks – USA

Warum Nationalparks wichtig sind:

Erster Nationalpark in den USA:

Standort des ältesten Baums:

Genaue Position des ältesten Baums ist geheim, weil:

Höhe des Mount Denali in Alaska:

A big country

4

Use an online map to find out the distances between different places in the USA. Complete the table.

from ... to ...	distance in miles	distance in km	distance in hours (by car)
Portland to Philadelphia			
Los Angeles to San Diego			
Miami to Minneapolis			

Getting around Bavaria

5 skill: writing TB p. 165

Write a message to Sarah in the USA about how people like to travel in your town or city. Tell Sarah about:

- how people can travel in your area (bike, bus, train ...)
- your favourite way to travel and why you like it
- an advantage and a disadvantage of your favourite method of transport

Don't forget to give some extra information and a personal comment. Write 60 words or more.

Whale watching

6 grammar: mixed grammar TB p. 161

Read the text about Sarah's whale watching tour. Fill in the gaps using the correct form of the verbs in brackets. You need all the tenses you have learnt so far: *simple present, present progressive, simple past, past progressive, present perfect*, the *will-future* and the *going to-future*.

Dusty explains
Look out for signal words to help you decide which tense you need!

Hello and welcome aboard the Pacific Explorer – I am your captain!

We ____________________ (leave) soon and I'm excited to share the incredible stories of the amazing creatures that live here with all of you.

Puget Sound is famous for its many different sea animals, and during our trips, we usually ____________________ (see) interesting species like orcas, humpback whales, gray whales, and the shy minke whales. A long time ago, Puget Sound ____________________ (be) an important waterway for Native American tribes.

Right now, our skilled crew ____________________ (get) the boat ready for our journey.

Please keep in mind that every trip is different, and we can't always predict how many orcas we ____________________ (see). Last week, while we ____________________ (sail), everyone on board ____________________ (get) to see orcas jumping out of the water. It ____________________ (be) really amazing to watch!

Already, scientists ____________________ (learn) a lot about the whales in Puget Sound.

They ____________________ (identify) specific orcas and have understood a lot about their families and social groups.

Today, it ____________________ (be) important to think about taking care of Puget Sound and the animals that live here.

In the next few months, we ____________________ (start) an educational program on the boat.

This ____________________ (help) everyone learn more about taking care of the ocean and the animals in Puget Sound.

Look! The crew ____________________ (give) me the thumbs-up for our departure.

Thank you for choosing the Pacific Explorer for your whale watching adventure.

More practice: listening

1a audio 2/38

You will hear five short conversations. Find out where the people are. Write the correct numbers (1–5) in the boxes. Use each number only once. Be careful, there are three boxes that you do not need.

☐ at the shopping mall ☐ on the bus ☐ in a coffee shop ☐ in the kitchen

☐ at school ☐ in a restaurant ☐ at the park ☐ at the supermarket

1b audio 2/39

You will hear Mikey, William and Jordan talking about the Super Bowl. Finish sentences 1–5 with the correct ending. Tick (✓) A, B or C.

1 Which team do Mikey and William think is best?

A ☐ The Chiefs
B ☐ The Eagles
C ☐ both teams are really good

2 What have the media been doing?

A ☐ supporting both teams
B ☐ guessing who will win
C ☐ supporting The Eagles

3 Why doesn't William like what the media were doing?

A ☐ it's making fans angry at the media
B ☐ it's making the players angry
C ☐ it's making the fans angry at other fans

4 How would Mikey feel if it was his first game?

A ☐ scared
B ☐ happy
C ☐ bored

5 What happens at the half-time show?

A ☐ the players are nervous
B ☐ the players sing
C ☐ famous singers perform

1c audio 2/40

Sophie wants to visit Olympic National Park. She calls the local tourist office to get the information she needs. Listen and complete questions 1–4. There is one example at the beginning (0).

Olympic National Park

0 **name of contact person:** *Madeleine*

1 **how to get there: (2 details)**
- ______
- ______

2 **opening times:** ______

3 **price with car:** ______

4 **price of annual pass:** ______

Check out

Speaking solutions p. 81

Talk to a partner. Tell each other what you are going to do at the weekend.

You can say:

On Saturday, I'm going to …
On Sunday, I'm going to …
Then I'm going to …
For breakfast, I'm going to …
In the afternoon, I'm going to …
In the evening, …

I can: talk about plans for the future. ◯

Reading solutions p. 81

Read Ashley's message to Robin. In which line(s) can you find the following information?

Hey Robin! The cleanup event was so cool! Amazing to see how many people wanted to take part! We got into groups and chose a name for our team. Cathy, Oliver, Liam, Sam and I called our team OCEAN'S 5. There was a competition: the team who collected the most trash won. Then we got our cleanup sets (gloves, trash bags and trash pickers), and Ms Moore told us we had to be extra careful and never touch anything with our hands. Then she shouted "GO!" and we were off. Four hours later everyone counted their trash bags. WE WON! 5 tickets to the movies!

1 Lots of people took part in the event: ______
2 There were 5 people in Ashley's group: ______
3 The teams were collecting rubbish: ______
4 The teams got special equipment: ______
5 The competition lasted a few hours: ______
6 Ashley's team had the most rubbish bags: ______

I can: understand a message about an event. ◯

Mediation solutions p. 81

Lies den Text. Vervollständige das *fact file* stichpunktartig auf Deutsch. Ein Wort genügt nicht.

American football was invented in the late 1800s, and the first college football game was played in 1869. Each team has eleven players. Players score points by getting the football across the other team's goal line. The team with the most points wins. A game usually lasts around three hours.
The Super Bowl is one of the most watched football events in the world. Companies pay a lot of money to advertise when the Super Bowl is shown: around 7 million dollars for 30 seconds!

FACT FILE
Wann erfunden:
Anzahl der Spieler pro Team:
Wie werden Punkte erzielt?
Wer gewinnt?
Typische Dauer eines Spiels:
Kosten für Werbung während des Super Bowl:

I can: understand relevant information in a text. ◯

Writing solutions p. 81

Look at the pictures. What happened? Tell the story. Write 60 words or more.

I can: write a picture-based story. ◯

Listening
audio 2/42, solutions p. 81

Listen to Matt talk about his school schedule. Find the mistakes in the sentences and correct them.

0 Matt's school day starts with ~~math.~~ *homeroom*

1 Matt's schedule is the same every day. ______

2 French is Matt's elective. ______

3 On Thursdays, Matt has Spanish in the morning. ______

4 Film Club is on Tuesdays. ______

I can: understand a text about US school life. ○

USE OF ENGLISH

Grammar
solutions p. 81

a) What are they going to do next? Write sentences. Use the *going-to future*.

0 Ashley: go to the movies with her friends *Ashley is going to go to the movies with her friends.*

1 Mr Turner: watch the Super Bowl ______

2 Robin: bake cookies ______

3 Terry and Sally: go hiking ______

b) Now write questions for the sentences in a). Use the *going-to future*.

0 *Who is Ashley going to go to the movies with?*

1 ______

2 ______

3 ______

Vocabulary
solutions p. 81

Fill in the gaps with the right words from the box. There are two words that you don't need.

hurricane · homeroom · cap · elective · cafeteria · lockers · states · gown · homecoming

1 In many schools in the USA, the day starts with ______ . That is where teachers check who is there.

2 When students graduate from high school, they usually wear a ______ and ______ .

3 Most students put their books and snacks in their ______ .

4 A school subject that students can choose is called an ______ .

5 Kansas, California and Florida are ______ .

6 A ______ is a very violent storm.

I can: write about plans for the future. ○ talk about things and places in the USA. ○

Check out – Unit 1

Speaking & Writing

Individuelle Lösungen

Listening

Listen to Tim. Tick (✓) all the things he did in the holidays.

- [x] spend a lot of time at home
- [x] go to London Zoo
- [ ] watch a film at the cinema
- [x] play volleyball at Hyde Park
- [ ] eat vanilla ice cream

Mediation

Lies dir das Schild durch. Ergänze die fehlenden Informationen im deutschen Infotext.

Beispiellösung:

Der Buckingham Palast hat *775* Räume. Im *Sommer* können Besucher den Palast besichtigen. Im Palast werden *Feiern* veranstaltet. Viele königliche *Kinder* wurden im Palast geboren.

Reading

Read Boris' postcard. Answer the questions about it. Take notes.

1. in London
2. It is sunny.
3. He thinks it's cool.
4. Buckingham Palace, London Eye, Hyde Park / lots of famous sights
5. shopping at Camden Market
6. to learn about history

Grammar

What did Melody do in the holidays? What didn't she do? Write sentences. Use the *simple past*.

1. She baked a cake. / She ate cake.
2. She didn't paint.
3. She didn't go to a museum / an art gallery.

Vocabulary

Sort the words and phrases in the box into the table.

holiday activities	weather words	directions	places in London
visit family	*cold*	*turn right*	*Hyde Park*
meet friends	*rainy*	*cross the street*	*Covent Garden*
go to the park	*warm*	*on the left*	*the Tower of London*

Check out – Unit 2

Speaking & Writing

Individuelle Lösungen

Listening

Listen to Terry. Find and correct the mistakes.

1 Terry and Louis had food from at least ~~10~~ different countries. *20*

2 The cake was made with chocolate and ~~cheese.~~ *zucchini*

3 It was interesting to learn about ~~Italian~~ cooking. *vegan*

4 Louis liked the ~~insects~~ best. *cheeses*

5 Terry and Louis are ~~not~~ coming back next year. *definitely*

Reading

Complete the text with the sentences (A–E). There are more letters than you need.

The most important rule is: never share personal information, online. You should also be careful when posting photos. [*E*] Always think before you post. Don't post a picture of someone else without asking them. [*A*] Imagine how you would feel! Always remember: [*D*] So when you comment on something be polite. [*C*] You can use emojis to help other people understand what you mean.

Mediation

Lies den Infotext über die *Big Issue*. Korrigiere die Fehler in den deutschen Sätzen.

Beispiellösung:

1 Man braucht ~~keinen~~ Termin, um anzufangen. *immer einen*

2 Verkäufer sollen ~~ihre eigene Kleidung~~ tragen. *Kleidung der „Big Issue"*

3 Verkäufer ~~kaufen~~ die ersten 10 Zeitschriften ~~zum halben Preis.~~ *bekommen / kostenlos*

4 Die Verkäufer verdienen ~~£4~~ pro Zeitschrift. *£2*

Grammar

What were the people doing last Monday at 4 p.m.? Fill in the verbs in the *past progressive*.

1 The chef was explaining how to make scrambled eggs from tofu.
2 Louis wasn't eating spicy insects.
3 We were talking about the "Big Issue".
4 My parents were asking about the school trip.

Vocabulary

<u>Underline</u> the wrong word and think of a suitable word for each line.

1 <u>vegan</u> – vegetarian
2 <u>jobless</u> – homeless
3 <u>hopeless</u> – hopeful
4 <u>eat</u> – post

Check out – Unit 3

Speaking & Writing

Individuelle Lösungen

Reading

Read the report and circle the correct answers.

1 They went there by: bus | train | plane.
2 The journey there took: 1.5 hours | 2 hours | 3 hours.
3 On the train they ate apples | sweets | chips.
4 They visited the Cadbury chocolate factory and: ate a lot of chocolate | learned how to make chocolate | talked a lot about chocolate.

Listening

Listen. Are the statements right or wrong?

1 The class met at Heathrow Airport. **wrong**
2 They went to Wales. **right**
3 They went to a very boring museum. **wrong**
4 It was a museum about ships. **wrong**
5 They also took a walk around the city. **right**

Mediation

Lies das Schild. Beantworte die Fragen stichpunktartig auf Deutsch. Ein Wort genügt nicht.

Beispiellösung:

1 in Edinburgh, Schottland
2 im Jahr 1955
3 altes Spielzeug, Spiele, Kleidung und Bücher
4 eine Puppe von 1740

Vocabulary

Circle the odd word out and explain your choice.

Beispiellösung:

1 museum – not a place to stay
2 coach – not a type of food
3 journey – not a means of transport

Grammar

a) What have they done on their trip? Write sentences. Use the *present perfect*.

1 Alice has eaten breakfast on the train.
2 They have seen colourful houseboats.
3 We have visited an open-air museum.

b) Write the correct *possessive pronouns* for the blue words.

1 mine
2 his
3 ours
4 yours / hers

Check out – Unit 4

Speaking & Writing

Individuelle Lösungen

Listening

Listen and tick (✓) the right answers.

1 Scotland
2 Edinburgh
3 about five hours
4 Aberdeen
5 around 1 p.m.
6 have lunch

Mediation

Lies den Infotext. Beantworte die Fragen stichpunktartig auf Deutsch. Ein Wort genügt nicht.

Beispiellösung:

1 Die Straße ist unterirdisch (und sehr eng).
2 Straßen wurden oft nach wichtigen Menschen benannt.
3 Mary King war eine erfolgreiche Geschäftsfrau.

Reading

Read the postcard. Then read the sentences and tick (✓) them right, wrong or not in the text.

1 The weather has been bad.	**wrong**
2 They are looking for Nessie at the moment.	**wrong**
3 They have already visited Edinburgh Castle.	**right**
4 They have not visited The Real Mary King's Close yet.	**wrong**
5 They have not tried haggis yet.	**not in the text**
6 Charlie loves Scottish music and dancing.	**right**

Grammar

Form sentences in the *present perfect*.

1 Gemma has already played the bagpipes.
2 Charlie has recently been to a ceilidh.
3 Sue and Gordon have cooked haggis for their family.
4 Mara has already finished her homework.

Vocabulary

Fill in the gaps with the right words.

1 wedding
2 lakes
3 tattie
4 century
5 book
6 Lad

Check out – Unit 5

Speaking & Writing

Individuelle Lösungen

Listening

Listen to the dialogue and answer the questions.

1 Amy
2 A point system for vegan and vegetarian food in the cafeteria.
3 It's a really good idea.
4 a vegan chocolate bar
5 talk to a teacher about the idea

Mediation

Mache dir stichpunktartig Notizen zum Poster auf Deutsch. Ein Wort genügt nicht.

Beispiellösung:

1 ein Monatsabo
2 10.000 Fahrräder
3 gar nichts / es ist kostenlos
4 $19 pro Tag
5 1000 Stationen

Reading

Read the email and answer the questions. Underline the answers in the text and write down the number.

Hi Jen,
Thank you very much for your email! You asked what I usually [0] do after school. Well, mostly I go to an after-[1]school club. On Mondays, there's Cooking Club. On Tuesdays, I go to the Theater [2] Club. And on Fridays, I've got Green Club. Do you have clubs at your [5] school? And if yes, do you have a favorite?
My favorite is the Theater Club. I also often meet my friends after school [3] or after the clubs. We go to the [4] movies or just hang out at the mall. What do you [5] do after school? Looking forward to your next message!
Best wishes, Oliver

Grammar

a) Fill in the right future form. Use *will-future, present progressive* or *simple present with future meaning.*

1 The school bus leaves at 7 a.m.
2 I think you will like the food there.
3 We are visiting my grandma tomorrow.
4 Oliver and his friends are going to the movies after school tomorrow.
5 The concert starts at 6 p.m.
6 It will be so much fun!
7 The friends are meeting this afternoon.
8 My mum thinks it will be too cold to meet outside.

b) Sort the sentences from a) into the table.

predictions / instant decisions	scheduled events	plans
I think you will like the food there.	*The school bus leaves at 7 a.m.*	*We are visiting my grandma tomorrow.*
It will be so much fun!	*The concert starts at 6 p.m.*	*Oliver and his friends are going to the movies after school tomorrow.*
My mum thinks it will be too cold to meet outside.		*The friends are meeting this afternoon.*

Vocabulary

Complete the sentences with the right British and American words.

1 chips 2 cinema 3 sneakers 4 holiday

Check out – Unit 6

Speaking & Writing

Individuelle Lösungen

Reading

Read Ashley's message to Robin. In which line(s) can you find the following information?

1 line 2
2 lines 3 and 4
3 lines 5 and 6
4 lines 6 and 7
5 line 10
6 line 11

Mediation

Lies den Text. Vervollständige das *fact file* stichpunktartig auf Deutsch. Ein Wort genügt nicht.

Beispiellösung:

Wann erfunden: **im späten neunzehnten Jahrhundert**
Anzahl der Spieler pro Team: **11 Spieler**
Wie werden Punkte erzielt? **Der Fußball muss hinter der Ziellinie des anderen Teams sein.**
Wer gewinnt? **Das Team mit den meisten Punkten am Ende des Spiels.**
Typische Dauer eines Spiels: **ca. 3 Stunden**
Kosten für Werbung während des Super Bowl: **$7 Millionen für 30 Sekunden**

Listening

Listen to Matt talk about his school schedule. Find the mistakes in the sentences and correct them.

1 Matt's schedule is the same ~~every day.~~
on Mondays, Wednesdays and Fridays

2 ~~French~~ is Matt's elective.
App development

3 On Thursdays, Matt has Spanish in the ~~morning.~~
afternoon OR ~~Spanish~~ – *art, PE and German*

4 Film Club is on ~~Tuesdays.~~
Fridays

Grammar

a) What are they going to do next? Write sentences. Use the *going-to future.*

1 Mr Turner is going to watch the Super Bowl.
2 Robin is going to bake cookies.
3 Terry and Sally are going to go hiking.

b) Now write questions for the sentences in a). Use the *going-to future.*

Beispiellösung:

1 Is Mr Turner going to watch the Super Bowl?
2 Is Robin going to bake cookies?
3 What are Terry and Sally going to do?

Vocabulary

Fill in the gaps with the right words from the box. There are two words that you don't need.

1 homeroom
2 cap / gown
3 lockers
4 elective
5 states
6 hurricane

Audiotracks

Unit 1 – Part A
1/1 **TB 1c** Check in – Tia's holidays
1/2 **TB 1b** Back to school
1/3 **TB 2** Visit Wales
1/4 **WB 3a** Emma's photos

Unit 1 – Part B
1/5 **TB 1a** This weekend
1/6 **WB 2a** Amy's trip to London
1/7 **WB 2** A sightseeing tour
1/8 **WB 3** Sights and sounds

Unit 1 – Part C
1/9 **TB 1b** The way to London Zoo
1/10 **WB 3a** Sound check
1/11 **TB 2b / WB 4** Which way?
1/12 **TB 1** Target Task – Create an audio guide
1/13 **TB** Check out – Reading
1/14 **TB** Check out – Listening
1/15 **WB** Check out – Listening
1/16 **TB** Check out – Mediation

Unit 2 – Part A
1/17 **TB 2** Check in – At the Tube station
1/18 **TB 1a** The "Big Issue"
1/19 **TB 3a** On the escalator
1/20 **WB 3** How to use an Oyster Card

Unit 2 – Part B
1/21 **TB 1a** The Brixton Food Festival
1/22 **TB 3** An interview

Unit 2 – Part C
1/23 **TB 1a** A funny photo?
1/24 **TB 2b** Social media
1/25 **TB** Check out – Listening
1/26 **WB** Check out – Listening
1/27 **TB** Check out – Reading
1/28 **TB** Check out – Mediation

Unit 3 – Part A
1/29 **TB 1b** Check in – One nation – four countries
1/30 **TB 1** Where can we go?
1/31 **TB 2a** A class trip

Unit 3 – Part B
1/32 **TB 1a** Welcome to Wales
1/33 **TB 2/5a** The last day of the trip / A discussion
1/34 **TB 3** Signs in Wales

Unit 3 – Part C
1/35 **TB 1b** Birmingham
1/36 **TB 3** What's on in Birmingham?
1/37 **WB 3a/3b** At a car boot sale
1/38 **TB 1b/1c** Culture – Around the UK
1/39 **TB** Check out – Reading
1/40 **TB** Check out – Listening
1/41 **WB** Check out – Listening
1/42 **TB** Check out – Mediation

Story
1/43 Kora and the New Zealand Dragons 1
1/44 Kora and the New Zealand Dragons 2
1/45 Kora and the New Zealand Dragons 3
1/46 Kora and the New Zealand Dragons 4

Unit 4 – Part A
2/1 **TB 1a** A video chat
2/2 **TB 2** Scottish English
2/3 **TB 3** A bagpipe workshop
2/4 **WB 4a/4b** A conversation

Unit 4 – Part B
2/5 **TB 1a** Welcome to Edinburgh
2/6 **TB 2** Burns supper
2/7 **TB 3** Scottish porridge
2/8 **TB 4a/3 WB 3** Have you ever ...? / A song

Unit 4 – Part C
2/9 **TB 1b** A trip to Loch Ness
2/10 **WB 2a** Did you know?
2/11 **WB 2b** Did you know?
2/12 **TB 1** Challenge – Scottish English
2/13 **TB 1c** Culture – Highland Games
2/14 **TB** Check out – Listening
2/15 **WB** Check out – Listening
2/16 **TB** Check out – Mediation
2/17 **TB** Check out – Reading

Unit 5 – Part A
2/18 **TB 1c** Check in – The USA at a glance
2/19 **TB 1a** Preparing for the United States
2/20 **TB 2** Stamford weather
2/21 **WB 5** A weather song

Unit 5 – Part B
2/22 **TB 1a** An email from Jack
2/23 **WB 3a** British or American?

Unit 5 – Part C
2/24 **TB 1a** A field trip to NYC
2/25 **WB 2** Tour of a green roof
2/26 **TB 3** Culture – Facts about the USA
2/27 **TB** Check out – Listening
2/28 **WB** Check out – Listening
2/29 **TB** Check out – Mediation
2/30 **TB** Check out – Reading

Unit 6 – Part A
2/31 **TB 1b** Check in – American school life
2/32 **TB 1a** A typical school day
2/33 **WB 3** Morning announcements

Unit 6 – Part B
2/34 **TB 1a** A super event
2/35 **WB 3** A phone call with a friend

Unit 6 – Part C
2/36 **TB 1a** A trip to the west coast
2/37 **TB 2** Going home
2/38 **WB 1a** Challenge – More practice: listening
2/39 **WB 1b** Challenge – More practice: listening
2/40 **WB 1c** Challenge – More practice: listening
2/41 **TB** Check out – Listening
2/42 **WB** Check out – Listening
2/43 **TB** Check out – Mediation
2/44 **TB** Check out – Reading

Audios

Tonstudio: 2020 Recordings, London; Directed by Stefan Szwarc, Sound Design by Rakel Pascual
Gesprochen von: Luke Francis, Ilan Galkoff, Emily Joyce, Helen Keeley, Dray Oliver, Nathaniel Priestley, Roisin Rankin, Zane Siddiqui, Ellis Sutherland, Maya Thomas und Sofia Thomas
Songs:
Track 2/8 (Textbook): Have you ever ...?; Music Tobias Friedrich, Berlin.
Track 2/21 (Workbook): A weather song; Music and vocals James Nicolau, London.

Videos

Miguel Amortegui, Changoman Productions, Brighton
Creative Listening, London
Tobias Ludwig, Wildfang, Berlin
Andrea Naumann, Aachen (Illustrationen Video 4)
Leonard Schwarz, Braunschweig

Bildquellen

|Alamy Stock Photo, Abingdon/Oxfordshire: Herrett, Roberto 34.2; Stainforth, Robert 26.2, 26.3; Threlfall, Hugh 34.4. |Alamy Stock Photo (RMB), Abingdon/Oxfordshire: Buckley, Drew 4.7; CW Images 4.8; Fotomaton 18.2; french, tony 30.4; International Photobank 4.9; Justin Kase zsixz 18.7; Kruse, Joana 41.5; one-image photography 13.2; robertharding 18.1; stock_wales 4.6; Sutton, Andy 32.1; WENN Rights Ltd 8.2. |Amortegui, Miguel, Brighton: 12.1. |Ellert, Mario, Bremen: 16.1, 20.1, 49.1, 70.1, 72.1, 111.1, 112.1, 113.1, 114.1. |Fast, Lisa, Hannover: 23.1. |fotolia.com, New York: Aleksandr Zholobov 38.3; Dar1930 30.8; Dario Sabljak 4.5; JFL Photography 30.6; ksena32 45.5; philip kinsey 38.6; Picture Partners 45.4; Tanja 30.9; Vermenko, Denis 30.7; viperagp 45.1; vladimirfloyd 43.3. |Getty Images, München: 2019 Horacio Villalobos - Corbis 64.1, 64.2, 64.3, 64.4, 64.5, 64.6, 64.7, 64.8, 64.9, 64.10, 64.11, 64.12, 64.13, 64.14, 64.15. |Götjen, Thomas: 8.1. |iStockphoto.com, Calgary: _ultraforma_ 18.4; andresr 18.6, 44.3; bukki88 Titel; Burt, Samuel 45.2; dibrova 59.1; FotografiaBasica 43.8; freeman98589 25.2; IR_Stone 18.3; JoeLena 44.1; Krasula, Milan 43.5; kris1138 30.1; Maxger Titel; nerudol 43.6; omersukrugoksu 52.1; pearleye 20.3; Pietrzykowska, Anna 71.1; sborisov 38.1; stockcam 45.6; taikrixel 13.3; Uhernik, Bruno 18.5; urfinguss 4.1; Valeriy_G 12.5; Vignjevic, Dobrila 12.3; Yobro10 62.5; zhuzhu 29.1. |mauritius images GmbH, Mittenwald: Science Source 25.6; Science Source / New York Public Library 25.4. |Naumann, Andrea, Aachen: 4.2, 4.4, 5.1, 5.2, 5.3, 5.4, 12.2, 12.4, 14.1, 14.2, 14.3, 14.4, 14.5, 14.6, 14.7, 14.8, 14.9, 26.1, 31.1, 31.2, 31.3, 31.4, 31.5, 31.6, 31.7, 31.8, 35.1, 35.2, 35.3, 40.1, 40.2, 40.3, 40.4, 41.1, 41.2, 41.3, 41.4, 46.1, 46.2, 46.3, 67.1, 67.2, 67.3, 68.1, 68.2, 68.3, 68.4, 68.5, 68.6, 74.1, 74.2, 74.3. |Shutterstock.com, New York: Bentlage, Henk 30.2; davooda 62.1, 62.2, 62.4; Dell 48.1; Everett Collection 25.5; Gin Tonic 20.4; lucianoxlima 44.6; stockcreations 20.2, 38.5; Whyte, Jeff 43.1; Zaitseva, Zoriana 4.3. |stock.adobe.com, Dublin: Andronov, Leonid 30.5; Cali6ro 59.2; chrisdorney 34.1; david@engel.ac 44.2; Divizia, Claudio 34.5; Dorin 43.2; dudlajzov 34.3; Eichhammer, Michael 44.5; fotolupa 13.1; G. Lombardo 44.7; Krakenimages.com 25.3; Kuttelvaserova, Vera 60.1; littlehandstocks 62.3; Mainka, Markus 45.3; mooseproductions 52.2; mrnai 38.2; Mucha, Thomas 25.7; Pixel-Shot 15.4; Pixeltheater 15.3; showcake 43.7; Trapp, Benny 44.4; Urupong 25.1; voltan 15.2; yanlev 15.1; Yaumenenka, Natallia 43.4; zinkevych 14.10; © 2013 Alfred Weintoegl, Gumpendorferstraße 36/35, 1060 Wien, all rights reserved 30.3; ©MosunoMedia 38.4.